PASSION OR PENALTY

A SWEET HOCKEY NOVELLA

D.C. EAGLES PREQUEL

LEAH BRUNNER

LEAH BRUNNER

COPYRIGHT

TRIGGER WARNINGS

This book contains themes of childhood trauma and anxiety.

PROLOGUE

MELANIE

THERE'S no time like the present to send your brother's best friend a recording of yourself expressing your undying love for him, am I right?

"Of course you're right. Do it," I whisper to myself, answering my own question.

Talking to myself? Wow, what the heck is in those pain meds the doctor gave me? I tap the camera app on my phone and press record before I lose my nerve.

"Heeeeeeeey, West!" I say to my phone screen. Noticing my normally well-kept hair is sticking up all over the place, I smooth it down with my free hand.

Usually, tangled hair would trigger my anxiety, but I currently feel more relaxed than I have in *years*.

"Thanks for the birthday text! Having appendicitis on your birthday sucks... but hearing from you made me feel better." A loud hiccup pops out of my mouth but I ignore it and continue, "I miss you and Harrison sooooo much!"

"Don't tell Harrison this, but I miss you more than him. I don't want to hurt his feelings... my brother is WAY more sensitive than he seems," I whisper the last part.

I'm feeling extraordinarily brave right now; maybe it's because I'm eighteen today and that means I'm more mature and stuff... or maybe it's just the anesthesia still wearing off from my emergency surgery.

"Anyway, everything was better when you lived right next door. I hate that you and Harry are away at college." A hiccup-laugh combo creates a loud squeak and I burst into giggles again.

"Don't tell him I called him Harry." I cup my hand over my mouth like someone is next to me and I don't want them to read my lips, even though I'm alone in my room. Mom thinks I'm taking a post-surgery nap.

I glance over at the large corkboard on my wall, which is filled with neat rows of concert ticket stubs and photos. Some of my friends have similar boards, but theirs are a mess of randomly placed photos and magazine clippings. Not mine. My photos are straight, and organized by the date they were taken. Most of the pictures are of me, Harrison, and West. The three musketeers. I yawn, exhaustion starting to make me sway.

"I'm sending you this video because..." I pause and stare into the eyes of West—the photo version on my corkboard—pretending he's right here in front of me. I'm a brave eighteen-year-old now. I can do this.

"Because I'm in love with you." I attempt a wink, but I think it looked more like a bug flew into my eye.

"It feels like there's something special happening between us. Like One Direction sings about in all their songs." I squint my eyes shut and try my hardest to recall some of the lyrics to my favorite One Direction song, "One Thing." I sing to the photo of West something about him being my kryptonite. I belt the song out passionately, at least the parts I can actually remember at the moment.

Honestly, my vocals are impeccable for how loopy I feel.

"So, for my birthday… I don't want to be the three muske-teers anymore. I want to be West and Melanie." I smile then gasp out loud when the best couple name pops into my head. "WESANIE! Do you like it? Oh my gosh, isn't it perfect?"

I smile at the screen before kissing it, picturing West's lips instead of my cold phone screen. It's covered with drool when I pull back, and I wipe it off with the weighted blanket on my bed. I can't think of anything else to say so I end the recording. Without even replaying it, I text it to West's number.

He's going to love it. I know he and Harrison made that stupid pact that they'd never date each other's sisters, but that was years ago! I'm basically an adult now. I can vote, get a tattoo, and smoke cigarettes (not that I'd ever do that). So dating my brother's best friend definitely isn't off the table.

I'm an adult and the world is my oyster.

––––––

"Melanie? Sweetie?" My mom's voice wakes me from the strangest dream. She rubs my back with her hand and smiles.

I blink a few times because she's so out of focus, it looks like there are five of her. My eyes don't seem to be working. I squint at the bright light coming in through my window; last I remember, it was dark out.

"What day is it?" My voice comes out in a croak.

Mom chuckles, her shoulder-length hair and large round eyes are starting to come into focus. "You had to have surgery yesterday, and you were pretty out of it from the anesthesia. Although very entertaining."

I begin to sit up in my bed but groan when the soreness in my abdomen hits me.

"You poor thing, let me help." My mom gently grabs my

arm and helps me sit up and rest against the headboard of my twin-sized bed.

She turns and grabs some pills and a glass of water she must've brought in with her. "Here, take these. They'll help with the pain. The doctor said you'll be sore for the rest of the week."

I rub my temples, trying to recall the events from yesterday. "It's so strange. I totally thought I dreamt the entire appendicitis debacle." Closing my eyes, I can smell the scent of lavender essential oils coming from my diffuser. Mom must've turned it on while I was asleep. "Wait, you said I'll be sore all week? What about swimming?"

Mom sighs. "I'm so sorry, but the doctor said no swimming for two weeks."

My eyes fill with tears. Swimming is one of the main activities I've found that eases my anxiety. My therapist encouraged me to face my fear of the water and swim several times a week. "But, Mom—" I start, but she interrupts me.

"I know it's going to be hard, but your body has to heal." She pats my blanket where my knee is, a loving look in her eyes as she tries to soothe me like I'm a little girl.

I choke back my tears and swallow the lump in my throat. "I just wish I was normal."

She gently puts her hand under my chin and nudges my face to look at her. "Melanie, there is nothing wrong with you. You're perfect just the way you are. There's not a person alive that doesn't have struggles and quirks."

"Not sure trauma-induced anxiety qualifies as a quirk," I tell her with a sassy expression on my face.

She wrinkles her nose. "True… but you *could* have irritable bowel syndrome like your father instead."

I laugh then grimace. "Don't make me laugh! And please never talk to me about Dad's bowels, gross."

She laughs. "All right, I'll try. Can I make you some breakfast?"

I nod, realizing I'm actually quite famished.

She grins, causing the lines around her eyes to scrunch up. My mom has a timeless beauty I've always admired. The kind of beauty that doesn't go away with age. With her shiny dark hair and big blue eyes, she reminds me a bit of Zooey Deschanel. I inherited my eyes from my mom, but I got my dad's lighter brown hair. If you ask me, it's kind of a mousy-brown color. I always wished I'd gotten Mom's dark brown color like Harrison did.

"I'll be back soon with some breakfast!" she tells me before cautiously sliding off my bed and leaving my room in the direction of the kitchen.

My head hurts so bad. I rub my temples again before reaching for my phone. I check my email and Facebook when I realize that I thought the appendectomy was a dream but it actually really happened—what if the rest of the dream was real too. I freeze, my eyes widening in horror.

"Oh. My. Gosh." I pull up my texts and tap on West's.

"NO. No, no, no!" I click on the video I sent him late last night and watch it. My face flames in humiliation. I exit the video to see if he's seen it yet; maybe he's still asleep. My eyes go to the corner of my phone where the time is displayed, 8:30 a.m. Shoot, he and Harrison will already be up and at hockey practice.

And sure enough, the read receipt shows *seen at 6:45 a.m.*

———

West

. . .

"You okay, West? You're acting weird."

My head whips over to look at my best friend, Harrison. "Me? Acting weird?" My voice comes out in a squeak, proving his point.

He quirks an eyebrow before settling onto his bed with a textbook. I sit on my own bed, which is across the room from his in our small dorm room. Posters of our favorite hockey players line the walls, and the room smells faintly of sweaty hockey equipment from practice.

No, our equipment isn't in our dorm; it's stored in the locker room. But somehow the scent lingers. Maybe from our socks?

Harrison is still looking at me curiously. I gulp, trying to think of an excuse for acting weird. I can't really tell him I'm filled with nervous energy because his little sister proclaimed her love to me with her words, and then again in song form. And I *definitely* can't tell him I reciprocate her feelings. That would defy the pact we made when we were thirteen.

There's one rule and one rule alone in our friendship: don't date each other's sisters.

It took me a few years to realize how unfair our pact was, seeing as my sisters are several years older than us and therefore completely uninterested in Harrison. Perhaps it's time to revisit the terms of this pact.

"I, uh, have a big test on Monday. Biochemistry." I grab my backpack from the foot of my bed and take out my chem textbook for good measure.

He doesn't look convinced but shrugs his shoulders and turns his attention to his homework. I breathe out a slow sigh of relief.

Harrison's phone pings with a text and his face scrunches up while he looks at the screen. "Ugh, poor Mel."

My eyebrows shoot up at the mention of Melanie, the girl

who has made my stomach flutter since I was old enough to notice girls. "Why? What's wrong?"

"Because of her appendectomy, she can't swim for a few weeks. She's freaking out about it."

My shoulders drop. I know how much swimming has helped her deal with her anxiety.

"I feel for the guy who ends up with my sister." He sighs.

Trying to keep my face neutral, I ask, "Why do you say that?"

"Ever since she fell through the ice on that pond when she was a kid, she has had this insatiable need to feel in control, or she has a panic attack. Her therapist told my parents she'd get better with time, but it happened *eight* years ago." He blows out a breath. "If she gets married someday, I feel like she's gonna need someone super reliable with a really tight schedule. Like a banker." He chuckles. "Definitely no one like us, pursuing pro hockey careers."

My breathing stops. "Yeah, true." I force a smile on my face and huff out a laugh.

Melanie's anxiety is directly related to her fear of ice and drowning, how could I ever be with her when my career is literally *on* ice. Not only that, but it would be really hard on someone who thrives on organization and consistency to handle the crazy schedule I'd have. My hockey coach has been talking to scouts and thinks I'll be drafted by the NHL sooner rather than later. Obviously, I'm thrilled about the possibility. I've worked my entire life to get to this point. But with training, practice, away games, late nights. I can't offer Mel any consistency at all.

My heart feels heavy at the thought that she might be better off with someone else. And it feels even heavier at the image of her with some faceless businessman. I don't even know him, but I hate this imaginary person.

I rake a hand through my hair, still wet from showering after practice, and remove my Bluetooth headphones from my backpack and turn them on. Leaning away from Harrison's view, I watch Melanie's video again, listening to her sweet voice through my headphones.

The rest of the day, I wrestle with my thoughts, but by the time the sun sets, I know what I have to do. I have to convince Melanie I don't feel the same way, even though it's a lie.

I'm no good for her; she'll be happier with someone else. And that thought kills me.

CHAPTER
ONE

I TAP my foot and glance at my watch while I stand in line waiting for my coffee order. This is not the morning to be late. Being a personal assistant to a member of Congress is a lot of pressure. Mr. Windell is probably the nicest politician I've ever met, but still, his wife is in town and I want to make sure everything is perfect.

Their favorite coffee shop is across town from my apartment, and despite leaving extra early this morning, I couldn't get D.C. traffic to cooperate with my perfectly timed plans. However, if the barista gets my coffee order for me in one minute and five seconds, I can still make it work.

My job is knowing everything, from Mr. Windell's coffee order to every second of his schedule. I'm here to make his life easier and his schedule seamless. And I'm damn good at it, if I do say so myself.

I was lucky enough to get this job straight out of college, and I will not, under any circumstances, mess it up.

"Melanie!" The barista finally calls.

Looking at my watch once more, I smile to myself. Nine seconds to spare.

I grab the coffee order, one Americano, and one plain black coffee. It's the most boring coffee order in the history of coffee orders. Mr. and Mrs. Windell are always very buttoned-up and straight-laced. But judging by the smirks and glances I catch between the two of them when they think no one is looking, I'm pretty sure there's a playfulness in both that they don't show in public.

"Thank you!" I tell the barista before turning and leaving the coffee shop.

After finally arriving at Mr. Windell's office twenty minutes later, I ride up the elevator and check my outfit in the shiny polished metal of the elevator. The pencil skirt is smooth, check. Pointed-toe heels looking chic but professional, check. White silk blouse buttoned up high enough to hide the goods, check. And, courtesy of a visit to the salon last week, my mousy-brown hair—which the stylist refers to as burnt sienna —is perfectly highlighted and blown out, check.

I'm ready and in the zone when the elevator dings and I stride into the small but lovely office space with confidence. Most buildings and homes in D.C. don't come with a generous amount of space, but they make up for it in charm. This building has been remodeled but still has that old world feel with the narrow windows and high ceilings. The windows allow in a generous amount of natural light, which, paired with the white walls and tile floors, makes the space bright and not dreary like a typical office.

I peek into Madden's office and find him sitting on his desk with his hands on his wife's waist while she stands between his legs and ties his tie. I hesitate before knocking, feeling like I'm interrupting an intimate moment.

But no one likes cold coffee.

I tap lightly on the door frame. "I hate to interrupt, but I have coffee." I smile and lift the drink carrier in my hand.

"Melanie, it's like you read my mind!" Mr. Windell stands and grins, showing off his perfect white teeth.

His wife turns on her heel to look at me, causing her brilliant red hair to fan out. She smiles at me before patting her husband on the chest. "So glad Madden has an amazing assistant to keep him caffeinated."

They grin at each other and I can't help but stare at them for a moment. Despite their boring taste in caffeinated beverages, they really are a stunning couple. Mr. Windell has chiseled features with wavy blonde hair that makes him look like he belongs in a Vineyard Vines catalog. And his wife is also gorgeous with her red hair, emerald green eyes, and round glasses. She reminds me a of sexy librarian slash fae princess.

I hand them the coffees and then turn to leave and walk back to my desk outside the office.

"Oh, Melanie!" Mrs. Windell calls.

"How can I help you, Mrs. Windell?"

She takes a few steps toward me. "Please, call me Odette."

Mr. Windells chuckles behind her. "Sweetheart, I've been telling her for a year to call me Madden and she still calls me Mr. Windell."

His wife places a gentle hand on my shoulder. "I appreciate your professionalism, but please call us by our first names. I insist."

Madden nods in agreement behind her.

I hesitate but then reply, "If that makes you both more comfortable, then Madden and Odette it is." I grin but feel a little weird calling them by their first names. Hopefully, I'll get used to it. They are, after all, only about ten years older than me.

Odette has a satisfied expression on her pretty face and pushes her glasses up higher on her pert nose. "Melanie, we'd love to take you out this week. I'm not in town very often now that we have the boys, but you work hard and I'd like to spoil you a bit."

"Oh, um, that's really not necessary—"

Madden interrupts, "Odette won't take no for an answer, trust me on this." He glances at his wife and winks at her. "We were hoping you might be free Friday evening for dinner? You're welcome to bring a date with you if you'd like."

I look down at my feet, feeling sheepish since Jeff and I broke up a few days ago. I quickly remind myself I'm an independent and self-sufficient woman and square my shoulders.

"It will just be me, but I'd love to have dinner with you both on Friday."

"Wonderful!" Odette claps her hands together. "I don't know if Madden told you, but I got my degree in political science as well, so we have lots in common."

A genuine smile tugs at the corners of my mouth. "Really? I didn't realize that. Well, I look forward to Friday." Odette smiles back at me and I turn my gaze back to my boss. "I emailed this week's schedule to you last night. Did you receive it . . . Madden?"

He smirks and crosses his arms. "See, calling me Madden wasn't so bad, now was it?"

I wrinkle my nose in response and they both laugh.

"Yes, I got the schedule and everything looks great. Thank you, Melanie," he says.

I take a few steps toward the door. "Great, let me know if either of you needs anything. I'll be at my desk."

They smile at me before turning back to each other. I catch a glimpse of Odette reaching for Madden's tie once again and straightening it for him.

CHAPTER
TWO
WEST

I WALK into my new house after a long and grueling hockey practice. After having the summer off, I couldn't wait to get back on the ice.

Hanging my car keys on the hook by the front door, I walk to the large window and admire the view from my new home. The foliage in Washington D.C. is beautiful this time of year, but I'm mostly excited that they don't get much snow here. After living in Quebec City for the last five years, I'm thrilled to have a break from the frigid weather.

My phone vibrates from the back pocket of my jeans, and I pull it out and see my best friend, Harrison, is calling.

"Hey, Harry," I answer with a grin, knowing he hates that nickname.

He scoffs. "I was about to ask how my favorite NHL player is settling in, but now I'm thinking you might be my *least* favorite NHL player."

I chuckle. "Sorry, man. I miss seeing the scowl on your face when I call you Harry though."

"Now that you live in the same city as my sister, you'll get to see that scowl more often."

I can hear the smile in his voice as he says it, but the reminder of Melanie makes my breath hitch.

"Ha, yeah." I try to disguise the nervousness in my voice.

"I'm actually coming to visit Mel in a few weeks. The three of us should hang out! It'll be just like old times."

"Uh, sure." I scratch my head. "I haven't seen Mel since last Christmas."

"Yeah, it's been difficult to get together with us all living in different cities. It'll be way easier now."

I realize I've absently been pacing in circles around my living room and stop, forcing myself to sit on my leather sofa. "Honestly, man, we haven't talked much since I got drafted back in college."

"Yeah, I noticed you guys barely talked at Christmas. What happened? You used to be so close."

Wiping my now sweaty palms on my jeans, I reply, "Well, college was busy with homework and practice... then I got drafted and moved to Canada." I take a deep breath and blow it out slowly. "I lost touch with a lot of people, Melanie being one of them."

The thought of seeing Melanie again makes my heart speed up like I just did skating drills for an hour.

"Oh," Harrison says, his voice laced with disappointment. "Well, now you guys are practically neighbors, so it's the perfect time to reacquaint yourselves!"

My shoulders tense. I know I hurt her all those years ago when I called her and told her I didn't feel the same way. It was such a lie, but she bought it so easily, which almost made it worse. She tried to convince me her recording meant nothing and she was just drugged up, but Melanie never says things she doesn't mean. I don't think even a drug-induced stupor could change that.

Harrison interrupts my thoughts. "Well, I know you probably just got home from practice, so I'll let you go. See you in a few weeks?"

"Yeah, man, can't wait." I smile; I've missed hanging out with Harrison, I'll see him way more now that we're in the same country.

I can hear him clear his throat through the phone. "Hey, try to keep an eye on my little sister for me, will you?"

With my free hand, I rub the back of my neck, which is now as sweaty as my palms. "Of course, I'd do anything for Mel," I answer honestly.

We hang up, and I sit on the couch staring blankly at the kitchen before closing my eyes. I picture Mel, with her hair color that's uniquely her, not quite brunette but not quite blonde. Something in between that just suits her perfectly. Her bright blue eyes that are so wide they always draw me in. And those kissable lips, like a cupid's bow, so pink and pouty. I've had dreams about kissing those lips way too many times.

I've never known what to do with my feelings for Mel, I always assumed they'd go away and I'd move on. But anyone I've ever dated has paled in comparison to her.

Maybe seeing her will be good. I've probably romanticized the idea of her after all these years. Only remembering the good things and not the annoying things about her... like how she has to schedule every moment of the day, or how meticulously she makes sure everything is straight and perfect, or how about how she always smells like essential oils??

We'll probably see each other as past acquaintances, and there won't be any spark between us at all. I mean it has been *five* years since we really hung out. Sure, we've seen each other in passing when we're home for the holidays since our parents still live next door to each other, but our interactions have remained surface level, the kind of conversations where you ask how the other is and you both reply, "good," then talk about the weather for a minute before excusing yourself.

She probably has a boyfriend too. My mouth twists at the thought.

With a deep sigh, I hoist myself up off the couch and trudge up the two flights of stairs to my large master bedroom. I go straight to my dresser, open the top drawer and pull out my old laptop from college. Making myself comfortable on my bed, I power on the computer and watch the video Melanie sent me when she was eighteen.

Yes, I saved it on my computer. No, I'm not going to admit how many times I've watched it.

I can't help but smile as I watch; this loopy version of Mel is so freaking cute. I pause the video after she says, *"I'm in love with you,"* and stare at her pretty face for a few seconds.

Slamming the laptop shut, I toss it away from me on the bed. Why do I torture myself like this?

I remind myself of the list of annoying things about Mel I mentally made earlier: schedules, neat-freak, essential oils.

Looking down at my luxurious king size bed that's now rumpled from my resting on it, I remember the heckling my teammates gave me about how much action this room is going to see.

If only they knew the only action this room will see is me sleeping. Alone. I've dated a lot of women, gorgeous women, sometimes models. But none of them have even come close to Melanie, the girl I've been pining over most of my life.

Closure. That's what I need. I'll hang out with Mel again in a few weeks and then I can move on with my life.

CHAPTER
THREE

MELANIE

AFTER COMING to the bottom of the steps in the D.C. metro, my heels screech to a halt. My face twists in annoyance as I take in the gigantic poster advertising the start of the D.C. Eagle's NHL season. The Eagles are a big deal here in the capital, but I've done my best to ignore anything hockey-related the past few years, thanks to a certain someone.

The same certain someone whose handsome face is staring back at me from the poster taking up an entire wall in the metro. Yep, Weston Kershaw just *had* to sign a contract with the D.C. Eagles once his time ended with the Quebec Wolverines. Here I've spent the past five years trying my best to avoid him, just to end up living in the same city.

Things became really awkward between us after I sent that video to him on my 18th birthday. He couldn't help that he didn't have feelings for me, but he didn't have to completely ghost me after telling me. Besides messaging each other happy birthday once a year, and having stilted conversations when we're both home for Christmas, we don't talk at all.

I heave an exasperated sigh as the metro arrives and rush to get on along with the rest of the crowd.

Why did he have to come to the same city as me? And *why* did they choose his face for the stupid poster, out of all the other players on the team? Okay, I know why. That chiseled jawline and messy blonde hair were made for a poster. The man is gorgeous, even more so now that he's a man and not a boy. Did he have to get better with age? The universe couldn't have given him early male pattern baldness or something?

I remind myself more than half a million people reside in D.C. So my chances of randomly running into West are slim. Not to mention he's a famous hockey player and we don't really hang out in the same circles. I'm so lost in thought, I nearly miss my stop but jump off the metro just in time.

I arrive at the office and take a seat at my desk outside Mr. Windell's—I mean, Madden's—office. I'm twenty minutes early, as usual. Madden's door is closed, which probably means he's on the phone. I walk to the small break room across from my desk and start a fresh pot of coffee. The aroma of the coffee brewing in the pot fills the entire office. I love the smell of coffee, but I don't drink it. I brew it purely for Madden's benefit.

While the coffee is brewing, I fill a mug with water and pop it into the microwave to heat up. I grab the small canister of herbal tea packets I keep here and select the lavender chamomile.

I learned years ago that my diet helps immensely with my anxiety. And when I stay away from sugar and caffeine, I sleep so much better at night. And luckily, it's been years since I had a nightmare about falling through the ice and drowning. My stomach churns at the reminder of the nightmare I used to have several times a week.

Shaking my head to urge those bad memories away, but a chill runs through my body. It's as if I can feel the sensation of water so cold it burned, like I'm stuck in that pond all over again. I sit back at my small desk and begging to distract myself from these thoughts by organizing my pens in alphabetical order by color. *Black, blue, orange, pink, red.* I repeat every color in my head and take deep breaths.

My anxious thoughts have dissipated enough that I power on my computer and double check Madden's schedule for the day. I call to confirm his appointments and make a note to pick up his dry cleaning. My job as an assistant may seem mundane to some, but keeping things orderly and on task eases my mind. As long as I keep myself busy, my mind doesn't have time to linger on whatever is triggering me at that moment.

The smell of coffee entices my boss out of his office, as usual. He opens his office door with a smile on his face. I notice for the millionth time that he has abnormally perfect teeth. I saw the Christmas card he received from his parents last year, which featured a photo of the entire family, and my jaw nearly dropped. The Windell family missed their calling as models. Seriously. I don't know how one family was so blessed genetically, it really isn't fair to the rest of us.

"Good morning," he says in a singsong voice before walking to the break room to pour himself a cup of coffee.

I can hear him humming to himself from the other room. He walks back into the main area, coffee mug in hand.

"Someone's in an awfully good mood today," I tease.

"Oh really?" He smiles. "Probably because Odette is in town. She puts an extra pep in my step."

I laugh and Madden walks closer to my desk so he can glance down at the notes I'm making on my tablet. "Don't worry about the dry cleaning; Odette is grabbing that for me today."

"Yes, sir," I say before erasing it from my calendar. "Any other changes?"

Before he can answer, we hear the office door open.

Madden's smile widens as he watches his wife walk through the door, and she smiles back at him just as big.

"How's the handsomest congressman in Kansas history doing today?" She says in a playful tone.

Madden brings his hand to his chest in mock offense. "*Kansas* history? Don't you mean the *nation's* history?" She rolls her eyes and laughs, and I snicker at their cheesy banter.

Odette is more casual today than I've ever seen her before, with her hair pulled back into a neat ponytail, white v-neck T-shirt, and slouchy boyfriend jeans. It's nice to see her dressed down, makes her seem more relatable.

"Did you tell Melanie the good news?" She looks from Madden to me.

"Oh, right! I forgot." He smirks. "Melanie, you're a hockey fan aren't you? Being from Minnesota and all?"

"Yeah, of course. I mean, I grew up watching my brother's games," I tell them with a smile—but leave out that they were also West's games.

"Wonderful!" Odette exclaims and claps her hands together.

Madden and Odette smile at me and I'm wondering if I should have inquired about why they needed to know if I was a hockey fan.

"There's been a slight change of plans for Friday evening," Madden says. "One of the Virginia state representatives has season passes for the D.C. Eagles, but he can't make the opening game on Friday—"

Odette interrupts, "So he gave us tickets to the game!"

My shoulders drop and I feel the blood rush from my face. They both look so thrilled at the idea of attending the game so I force a smile. "Wow, that's... great."

"This will be our first NHL game. I hope we see some

fights." Odette seems thrilled about the idea of seeing the hockey players throw some punches.

Madden laughs. "Yeah, this hockey thing is new to us. Hockey isn't really a thing in Kansas, we don't even have an NHL team."

My cheeks are beginning to hurt from my forced smile. "You guys will love it. Just the two of you should go! You know, make a date of it! I can have dinner with you another evening, I'm flexible." I'm trying to stay calm, but my voice sounds squeaky.

"No way, we need you there to explain the game to us." Odette winks. "And maybe one of those hockey players will catch your eye."

I feel the blood come rushing back to my face, I've probably gone from Edward the vampire to Mr. Crabs from SpongeBob in 0.5 seconds. "Sure, ha."

"So we'll leave straight from the office Friday and grab pizza first before heading to the game." Madden opens his mouth to say something else but his phone rings and he pulls it out of his suit pocket. "I better get this." He gives his wife a quick kiss then ducks into his office to answer his phone.

I glance down at my schedule before turning my attention back to Odette. "It's really no big deal if you'd like to go to the game with just Madden."

"That's sweet of you, but I've been hanging out with him all week!" She glances at Madden's closed door. "Well, I'll get out of your hair, I know you're busy. I'll text Madden that I headed out."

"Alright," I force a smile on my face, then pull my Bluetooth headset out of my top drawer and turn it on. "Text me if you change your mind."

"Sure thing. See you Friday!" She waves.

I wave back, but once she's out of sight, I allow my shoulders to drop. My stomach is in knots at the thought of not only going to an ice rink, but one of West's games? Ugh. I'm sure if I told them about my accident as a kid, they'd understand. But I've worked so hard to maintain my image of independence and professionalism. I don't want either of them to see me as a weakling.

———

Late that evening, I arrive home at my apartment. I can tell my roommate, Noel, is already home from work because her shoes and handbag are strewn haphazardly in front of the entryway. With a sigh, I place her shoes on the shoe rack and hang her bag on the hook before doing the same with my own.

"Mel? Is that you?" Noel calls.

"Honey, I'm home!" I yell back in a deep baritone voice, or at least as deep as my voice will go.

She meets me in the hallway with her hand to her chest and bats her long black eyelashes at me. "Oh my, is that you, Walter? How I've missed you today." She backs up against the wall and raises one leg in a sexy pose.

"You're taking the joke too far." I shake my head but laugh.

She laughs with me and pushes herself off the wall to give me a hug. "How was your day, roomie?"

"It was… interesting." I pull out of her embrace and continue down the hallway and into the kitchen.

She follows me, pulls some Chinese takeout leftovers out of the fridge, and pops them into the microwave.

Our kitchen is like the rest of our apartment: cute upon first glance, but once you look closer, you can see everything is a little old and worn. The countertop looks like a wooden chopping block, but it's just contact paper with a wooden pattern. The cabinets are white but the paint is chipping. And there's just enough room for us both to stand in here; as long as we don't make any sudden movements, we won't crash into each other.

Her eyebrows raise in curiosity. "Okay, this kitchen is now the Boston Harbor and it's 1773. So spill the tea."

I cock my head to the side to look at her with a pained expression. "Your history nerd is showing, you might want to tuck that back in."

"I'm a history professor; you know I can't help myself." She shrugs. "Quit stalling and tell me what's up."

I hesitate, considering if I want to give her all the details. Finally, I sigh and slump down on our tiny sofa. "You remember I'm from Minnesota, right?"

She nods. "Yes, the arctic tundra. I remember."

"Well, what I haven't told you is that our next-door neighbor's had three kids. Their youngest was the same age as my brother. And the three of us were really close... like we hung out all the time. I went to every single one of their hockey games and practices growing up."

"Keep talking," she urges as she shoves a large bite of orange chicken into her mouth.

"Well, I had a huge crush on the neighbor boy, West, and on my 18th birthday I had to have my appendix removed and was all loopy on pain meds."

She scrunches up her nose and swallows her bite. "Okay, you lost me with the appendicitis."

Grabbing a fork from a drawer and one of the Chinese containers, I begin to stir the fried rice around before continuing. "While I was drugged-up, I sent West a video of myself expressing my love for him."

Noel's jaw drops. "You didn't!"

I take a deep breath, remembering the dread I felt when I realized I'd actually sent that video and not dreamt it.

I slump back against the cabinet and take a bite of my rice. Noel nudges my shoulder from where she's standing next to me. "So what happened next??"

"Oh, right," I say around a mouthful of rice. I swallow then start again. "He called me and told me he didn't have feelings for me. Then he completely stopped talking to me for months."

"Wow. What a jerk." She settles back into the couch then furrows her brow. "But what does any of that have to do with you having an interesting day today?"

"Did I mention West went to college on a hockey scholarship?"

She shakes her head from side to side, making her blonde curls bounce.

"Well, he did. And he was drafted by the NHL. And this summer, he signed a contract with the D.C. Eagles." I stare at her to see her reaction, knowing how crazy this all must sound.

Her brown eyes widen. "Your childhood neighbor was Weston Kershaw??" she shouts.

"Would you keep it down?" I whisper-yell. "You know how thin these walls are!"

She grimaces. "Sorry."

"Yes, Weston Kershaw is my brother's best friend." I take a deep breath and blow it out slowly, causing my curtain bangs to fly up. "And I agreed to go to dinner with the Windell's Friday evening. But they got tickets to the Eagle's game, which means I have to be near *ICE* and I'll be at *West's* game."

Noel blinks rapidly a few times and purses her lips. She looks deep in thought, probably mulling over the details I just relayed to her. "Okay, this is fine. Not a big deal!"

I narrow my eyes at her. "Really? That's all you've got?"

"No, really. Listen, the Windells probably have fancy box

seat tickets. Which means Weston Kershaw will never even notice you're there, and you'll be far away from the ice."

"Oh my gosh, just call him West." I roll my eyes. "How'd you even know who he was, anyway? I thought you hated sports."

"Oh, I believe there are much better ways to spend one's time than playing sports. Participating in the arts, reading, brushing your teeth…" She's holding up a finger for each item on her list.

I cross my arms across my chest. "Okay, I get it."

"But sadly, several of my students are obsessed with him. Which is the only reason I know who he—or any other athlete for that matter—is." She shakes her head, a disgruntled expression crossing her face. "Anyway, back to the game. There's no way he'll even know you're there. I'm more worried about your anxiety."

"I'm hoping I'll be okay with the ice thing. The logical part of my brain knows I can't fall through an indoor ice rink… not to mention, I won't even be on the ice."

"Okay, but if you need me, just text and I'll be there," Noel says as she pats my shoulder.

"Oh, and if West happens to see you, who cares?" She shrugs one shoulder. "You're a confident, beautiful woman. You have a cute boyfriend, a job you love, and the best roommate a person could ask for."

I grimace. "All of that is true, except Jeff and I broke up."

"Oh my gosh, finally." She breathes a sigh of relief.

"You didn't like Jeff?" I asked, feeling surprised because Jeff is the nicest person ever.

She scoots closer to me and drapes an arm around my shoulders. "Of course I liked Jeff. Who wouldn't like him? The guy is a saint." She wrinkles her nose. "But the two of you acted like very well-mannered siblings. There was no chemistry whatsoever."

I worry my bottom lip. "Yeah, you're right. I wanted there to be chemistry so bad. He was just so *nice*."

"You can't spend your life with a man you have *nice* feelings for," she tells me with a smile.

I nod my agreement and we finish our Chinese food.

"Oh! Let's cyberstalk West!" Noel exclaims, making me jump.

"Please no. You'll just find a bunch of photos of him posing next to models." I groan.

She quirks a brow. "So you've stalked him before?"

"I don't have to; we're friends on Facebook so I get to see every photo he's tagged in."

Noel runs out of the kitchen and down the hallway toward her room, and returns with her laptop a few seconds later. She grabs my arm and drags me to the couch where we plop down.

I shake my head as I watch her type *Weston Kershaw* into the search bar. The first photo that pops up is one from his photoshoot with Sportsnet. He's shirtless and sitting on a Zamboni. His chest and arms are oiled up, showing off his chiseled body and his hair is tousled to perfection.

"Wow, he's a beautiful male specimen, huh?"

I lean forward and tap on the next photo, which is of West and a gorgeous woman. "A beautiful male specimen who has an unending conveyor belt of leggy models to date."

We spend the rest of the evening looking through photos of him, trying to find unflattering ones. There aren't any.

CHAPTER
FOUR
MELANIE

THE REST of the week has gone by much faster than I wanted it to. It's now the day of dread: Friday.

Noel's pep talk has completely worn off, and I've dealt with a headache and a queasy stomach off and on all day.

This morning, Madden even asked if I was feeling alright. He said I looked tired. Just what every woman loves to hear. I briefly considered feigning illness to get out of going tonight, but being dishonest just doesn't sit right with me.

A little after five p.m., Odette walks into the office. Despite it being a fairly warm October day, she's wearing a red Eagles jersey and matching knit hat complete with a pom-pom on top. She's grinning so big her cheeks are pushing her glasses up. I can't help but smile at her excitement. I supposed I'd be pretty thrilled too if this was my first NHL game.

Madden must've heard his wife come in and opens his office door. He chuckles as he takes in her ensemble. "Well, look at my sporty little wife. I could get used to this."

She blushes and hands him a jersey she has draped over her arm. "Here's yours. Go ahead and get changed." He kisses her cheek before grabbing the jersey and ducking back into his office.

Odette glances over at me. "Melanie, did you bring a change of clothes?"

I look down at my black trousers, leather flats, and pink blouse. "I'll be fine. I packed a coat to bring with me."

Madden comes out of his office looking very pleased with himself. All he's done is remove his suit jacket and replace it with a jersey; his collared shirt and tie are peeking out slightly above the jersey collar. I stifle a giggle as he walks toward his wife.

That's when I notice the name on the back of his Eagles jersey. *Kershaw*, with West's number, twenty-two, emblazoned on the shoulders. Madden hugs his wife and I see her jersey matches his.

I swear under my breath and have to grind my teeth together to keep myself from bringing my palm up to smack myself in the forehead. If we end up on the Jumbotron tonight, I swear I will die of embarrassment on the spot.

Madden and Odette turn to me, and Madden rubs his palms together. "Alright, who's ready for pizza?"

I gulp and try my best to smile.

———

Eating pizza was a horrible idea. I should've gotten a grilled chicken salad with oil and vinegar dressing to offset my nerves. My nerves are currently at the level of Elizabeth's mother in the movie *Pride and Prejudice*.

We're entering the arena and my brain feels fuzzy with anxiety. The crowds of people aren't helping either.

I tried to be present in the conversation during dinner, but I can hardly recall what we even talked about. Madden and Odette are blissfully unaware of my near-panic attack, holding hands and grinning. We walk toward the steps and I expect them to take the stairs going up, where the box seats would be. But to my horror, they start going down instead. I take a deep breath, reminding myself they've never been to a game and probably don't know how to find their seats.

"Hey," I call to Madden. "Do you need help finding our seats?"

He glances back at me, a look of confusion passing over his face. "I don't think so, this should be the right way." He turns and continues walking.

We keep walking down closer and closer to the ice, and with every step, my body becomes more numb. We don't stop until we're all the way down near the front row, right in front of the plexiglass.

"Here we are!" Madden announces.

They both take their seats and smile up at me. I hope my face doesn't mirror the embarrassment and dread taking over my body.

"Can you believe we get to sit in the front row?" Odette asks. She looks legitimately thrilled about it.

Closing my eyes for a second, I force myself to take a steadying breath before opening them again. "Yeah, these are great seats."

I take my seat next to Odette and turn to rummage through my handbag. I don't actually need anything out of it, I just need a moment to distract myself and gain some composure. Thankfully, we missed the warmup when the players come out and interact with fans. Once the game starts, they're too focused on the game to pay attention to the people in the stands.

Yes, this is going to be okay. This is fine. I'm *fine*.

A few minutes before puck drop, the lights in the arena dim, a spotlight shines where the players will come out, and "Thunderstruck" by AC/DC blares through the speakers. As they announce each Eagles player, the crowd goes wild. West is the last one to skate onto the ice and gets the loudest applause.

West was one of the top goal-scorers in the NHL last season, so as much as I hate to admit it, he's a pretty freaking big deal.

The group of women sitting directly behind us is going wild, whistling and calling West's name. I roll my eyes in annoyance then peek over my shoulder at the women and see they're holding large signs. One sign reads, "#22, will you marry me??" another says, "Future Mrs. Kershaw." There are hearts and red lipstick kisses all over the signs. The women reek of perfume and desperation.

The opposing team, the Raleigh Renegades, are announced with much less fanfare and then the game begins.

During the first period of the game, my body begins to relax. Halfway through the second period, I'm almost feeling normal again. We're over halfway through and West hasn't looked this way. And the Jumbotron hasn't zeroed in on us once. Whew.

The score is 3-1 in favor of the Eagles. Two of the goals were, of course, scored by West. This might make me a horrible person, but I'm praying he doesn't get a hat trick tonight. I don't want to listen to the women behind me oohing and ahhing more than they already are.

By the time the third and final period starts, I'm actually enjoying myself. I forgot how much fun it is going to hockey games. The sounds of the blades on the ice, the chill in the air, it's not only soothing to me but also nostalgic. I haven't skated since my accident when I was a kid. But maybe I could try skating again, indoors—you can't fall through the ice indoors, afterall.

How ridiculous was it that I was dreading tonight so much? Like an inch of ice is scary, or Weston Kershaw is going to pick me out of a crowd. Ridiculous.

I'm startled from my thoughts when I hear a loud crash. There's a sudden commotion in front of me. Two large hockey players have collided against the plexiglass directly in front of our seats.

I blink a few times, feeling stunned. I look at the men tangled up in front of me and meet the all-too-familiar grey eyes of West. His eyes lock on mine and I can see the moment realization dawns on him and he recognizes me.

Everything around me goes silent, and I can hear my pulse beating rapidly in my eardrums. The terrifying sensation of a panic attack begins to make its way throughout my body. All I want to do is run from this building and avoid the embarrassing memories associated with West. My brain instantly goes to the darkest place it can, back to being trapped under the ice. The chill running through my body, the glare of light coming from above the ice, the muffled voice of my brother calling for me.

I can't seem to move or even blink, and West holds my gaze for what feels like a long, frozen moment in time but was probably like three seconds. However, even three seconds is a long time when you're in the middle of a fast-paced hockey game.

His opponent easily steals the puck away from him while West stands there looking stupefied. When he finally snaps out of his stupor, he follows his opponent, trying to get the puck back.

The other team manages to keep possession of the puck

and scores another goal. The crowd groans, but I'm just sitting there in shock.

My body still feels numb, so I close my eyes and remember the words of my therapist from high school. *Count to three and take a deep breath, then repeat until you feel more calm and rational.* I breathe in through my nose, then out through my mouth slowly several times.

Odette leans in and whispers, "Are you alright?"

I nod my head yes.

She places a hand on my shoulder, her eyebrows drawn together in concern. "Those guys must've really scared you when they crashed into the plexiglass; you look pale."

"Yeah, ha. It kind of freaked me out. I'll be fine." My voice comes out in a whisper.

Odette rubs my shoulder in a comforting gesture, which is what my mom used to do when I was anxious. I find the touch surprisingly comforting considering I don't know Odette that well.

The game ends and the Eagles manage to win by one point. As soon as the buzzer goes off, indicating the end of the game, I jump up from my seat. I turn to exit our row—the sooner we get to the car, the sooner I can regain some sanity.

"Woah, not so fast!" Madden calls over the noise of the crowd. "I must've forgotten to tell you, but the Eagle's general manager found out we were coming tonight and invited us to meet the team afterward." He grins, and Odette does an excited little dance.

It takes every ounce of self-control left in my body to force a smile on my face. I'm sure it looks strained, but it's the best I can muster up right now. I sit back in my seat and internally lecture myself for not driving separately. My car is back at the office and I have no means of escape. I think about texting

Noel, but I'm twenty-three years old, I shouldn't need to be rescued.

CHAPTER
FIVE
WEST

SHE'S HERE.

I was not expecting to see her, and there she was, right on the other side of the plexiglass. Close enough I could have reached out and brushed my hand over her dewy skin. Meeting the gaze of those round blue eyes threw me off my game, and not just for the few seconds I stared at her in shock. I was off my game for the rest of the final period.

My teammates and I make our way back to the locker room, everyone high-fiving and celebrating our win. The Eagles' locker room is much nicer than the one in Quebec. They dressed it up with dark-stained wood and a large rug featuring our Eagle mascot. The ceiling is even lit with a giant light fixture in the shape of an eagle head. But no amount of lights and details can disguise the fact that it's a locker room, and it smells like Shrek's feet.

My mind drifts back to my lack of finesse during the final period and I slump down in my seat, hanging my head in shame. I not only choked in front of my new teammates but also Melanie. How embarrassing.

"Kershaw, what was your problem out there?" Mitch

Anderson, whose locker is next to mine, asks, his voice laced with anger.

Coach Young interrupts before I can answer. "That's enough, Anderson. Kershaw scored two goals tonight; how many did *you* score?"

Mitch doesn't speak, and the entire team is staring at me now.

I run my hands through my sweat-soaked hair. "Sorry about that final period, boys. I don't know what got into me."

Colby Knight, who's seated on my other side, speaks up. "When you came back from getting slammed up against the glass, you looked rattled. Are you injured?"

"Physically, no," I mutter under my breath.

"Don't sweat it, Kershaw. You're all still learning to play together; it was the first game and you guys did great. We'll learn from our mistakes and do better next time." Coach tells us before walking closer to me and giving me a friendly smack on the shoulder.

"Thanks, coach."

Coach puts his fists on his hips and glances around the room. "Okay, boys, get comfortable but stay decent. A congressman and his wife are coming back to meet the team."

Mitch groans next to me. I swear this guy is always in a bad mood. The rest of us remove our jerseys and some of our pads but keep our undershirts on. Just enough to cool down without giving the congressman's wife too much of a show.

If it wasn't for our fanbase, we wouldn't be here. Greeting fans is part of the job, and I don't mind it. Being recognized constantly and asked for autographs can get annoying some days, but there's nothing better than making someone's day by giving them a puck or posing for a selfie.

Our GM, Tom Parker, walks into our locker room and taps

his fist on the wall a few times. "Everybody decent? Our guests are here."

Coach Young glances around the room. "Yep, we're all good in here, Tom!"

Tom and Coach Young could pass as brothers, both are tall and lean with dark hair that's turning grey at the temples. Tom has blue eyes though and Coach has brown. They even tend to dress similarly. Tonight they're both wearing black suits with red ties.

I look between the two of them. "Do you two call each other ahead of time and plan this?"

Coach Young rolls his eyes. "It's not my fault Tom is always copying me. Probably since I'm so stylish."

Tom laughs. "Yeah, sure. *I'm* the one copying you." He shoots coach an over-exaggerated wink. "I'll go grab our guests." Tom smiles and leaves for a few seconds before coming back.

I'm expecting two people: the congressman and his wife. But there's a third person hiding behind the couple.

"This is Madden Windell, one of the state representatives from Kansas. And his lovely wife, Odette." Tom places a hand on Madden's shoulder.

They're much younger than I was expecting, maybe thirty? Madden looks to be just as fit as the guys on our team, and his wife is pretty.

"Tonight was our first time attending a hockey game and it was awesome. Great work, guys! We're fans for life now." Madden tells us with a wide grin, showing off a set of perfect teeth. Some of the guys in this room would kill for a set of teeth like that.

Tom introduces Coach Young and all the guys on the team. Madden starts looking around like he lost something, then glances behind him to the third person.

He laughs. "Don't be shy! Get out here and say hello." He and his wife gently drag the person standing behind them forward, and my heart stops at the sight of Melanie.

"This is my assistant, Melanie." He introduces her and the team comes forward to shake her hand.

When it's my turn, I step forward toward her. It feels like everything is happening in slow motion; I'm so nervous. I take her tiny hand in my large one and we stare at each other. Her cheeks are red with an enticing blush and her big blue eyes—they've always reminded me of a cartoon princess—are studying me. She's the same petite, beautiful girl I grew up with. But now she's all woman with an hourglass figure that can't be hidden by the pink cardigan she has draped over her delicate shoulders.

"Hey, West," she says quietly, drawing my attention to her perfect cupid's bow lips.

I force myself to move my attention from her mouth to her eyes, and what magical eyes they are.

"Hey, Mel. Good to see you." I choke out, hoping my voice doesn't betray how affected I am by her unexpected presence.

Realizing I'm still grasping her hand, I drop it and take a step back.

Madden and his wife look from me to Mel a few times before Odette asks, "Do you two know each other?"

She looks genuinely shocked, so It's obvious Mel hasn't mentioned to them that she knows me. For some reason, that makes me feel a little disappointed.

"West is friends with my brother," Melanie says with a forced smile.

Noticing she didn't say I was *her* friend as well makes my stomach drop in disappointment again.

"We were next-door neighbors." I add, "The three of us were inseparable growing up. Me, Mel, and Harrison." I smile and hold her gaze. The thought of how little we've talked the past few years makes my stomach churn.

"Yep, the three musketeers." She smiles back at me and there's sadness in her eyes. Or maybe I'm reading into it.

Everyone else in the room has lost interest in me and Melanie, starting up other conversations and autographing the Windell's jerseys. But I can't take my eyes off of the woman before me. I was a moron to think the connection between us would go away or that eventually I wouldn't be attracted to her. Even the few times I've seen her the past few years, there's still been a spark there, no matter how awkward and stilted our brief conversations were.

My mind swirls with thoughts of how much I've missed our friendship and all the things I've always loved about her... like how scheduled she is, and that she's so organized. But my favorite thing is that she always smells like essential oils.

Wait, wasn't that supposed to be my list of things that were annoying about her? Who was I kidding; they're not annoying qualities at all.

It was horrible of me to basically stop talking to her after she sent that video. I know I'm not her favorite person in the world—at least, that's what I've assumed from her body language every time I've seen her since. But at the time, I didn't know how else to keep my feelings for her at bay.

"Hey, we should catch up. Would you want to grab coffee this weekend?" I'm hoping if I ask her in front of all these people she won't say no.

She shifts her eyes around the room. "Um, sure. Okay."

Before I can say anything else, Madden and Odette ask me to autograph their jerseys. I realize for the first time they're wearing Kershaw jerseys and feel bad for not noticing sooner. But being so close to Melanie made me lose my bearings.

What am I going to do if she continues coming to my

games? I won't even be able to think. Maybe I can ask her not to sit in the front row.

Madden thanks Tom for inviting them to meet the team and then thanks us for the autographs. They say goodbye then begin to head towards the door.

"See you later, Mel." I nod my head in her direction.

She glances at me over her shoulder. "Bye, West."

She says it like it's final. As if she's not planning on seeing me again. But boy is she wrong. I'll do anything I can to at least get her to have coffee with me.

I head back to my locker and start removing the rest of my gear.

Mitch looks over at me with a smirk. He raises one eyebrow and says, "Wow, your friend's sister is a hot piece of—"

I get right in his face, fisting my hand in the front of his jersey. Anger is pulsing through my veins, making my skin feel like it's on fire. "If you finish that sentence, you're going to be missing a few more teeth."

Mitch throws his hands up in defense but looks amused. "Alright, alright. Get off me."

The rest of the team is staring at us. I narrow my eyes at them, and they return to removing their gear. I'm hoping they all got the hint that making comments about Melanie will cause punches to be thrown.

———

The next morning, I call the number I had for Melanie from high school.

A man who sounds elderly answers, "Hyellow?" His greeting sounds like a combination of *hellow* and *yellow*.

"Um hi. I think I might have the wrong number." I purse my lips.

"What was that?" he yells into the phone.

"I think I have the wrong number," I tell him, raising my voice slightly.

"You need some long lumber?" he asks, sounding even more confused.

I don't want to hang up on him and be rude, so I try once more. "No, I have the wrong number."

"I'm sorry, I don't know a gong plumber," he replies, sounding annoyed. "I think you have the wrong number." Then he hangs up.

I release a heavy sigh. This means she's gotten a new number, and I have no choice but to ask Harrison for it. I could message her on Facebook like I do every year on her birthday, but for some reason, that feels impersonal. And I really want to mend our relationship.

With a deep breath, I type out a text to Harrison.

WEST

> Hey man, can I have Mel's new number?

I pace the room waiting for his reply. Me and Melanie are grown adults. If I want to take her on a date, he can't do anything to stop me. I mean, that stupid pact we made was like fifteen years ago.

HARRISON

> New number?

WEST

> Yeah, I still have her old number from high school; we usually just message on Facebook.

I'm making it sound like we chat way more than we actually have.

HARRISON

Oh, sure, I'll send it over.

He shares her contact information with me and I save it into my phone.

CHAPTER SIX

MELANIE

"A *DATE*?!" Noel exclaims after I catch her up on the events from last night.

"No! He said he wants to *catch up*." I use my hands to make air quotes.

Noel does an excited little bounce and releases a squeal of delight. "This is the most excitement I've had since a boy in my class asked a girl to prom by singing her Michael Bolton's "When A Man Loves a Woman" in front of the entire class."

"Wow, we're circling back to that story in a minute." I smirk. "But I don't have to worry about actually catching up with West because he only mentioned it to be polite." I smile and raise my chin in smug satisfaction.

Her shoulders drop. "Well, that's no fun. I really wanted to hear all about this coffee date."

"Sorry, you'll just have to get your drama from your students."

My phone pings from the pocket of my fluffy pink robe. I take my phone out and see there's a text from a random number. I tap on it assuming it's some kind of spam.

UNKNOWN NUMBER

Hey Mel, it's West. Got your number from Harrison.

I gasp and nearly drop my phone. Noel comes to my side and reads over my shoulder.

"Oh my gosh! He's totally into you." She winks.

"Don't wink at me, it's creepy. What should I say?"

Noel moves directly in front of me and puts her hands on my shoulders. "Okay, take a deep breath and answer a question for me."

Closing my eyes, I take a deep breath.

"Tell me," She pauses and rubs my shoulders in a comforting gesture. "when you saw West last night, did you still feel something for him?"

I huff and scowl at her. She holds eye contact and gives me a knowing look.

With a sigh I say, "Alright… yes I still felt a spark. But he's not interested in me like that."

"Maybe this is a second chance. Feelings can change, you know." She waggles her eyebrows.

"I don't know, I don't want to get my hopes up. But… it would be nice to be friends again."

Another text comes through and Noel rushes back to my side so she can read over my shoulder.

WEST

So, would you be free to get coffee today or tomorrow? I don't have practice until this afternoon and have the day off tomorrow.

Noel claps her hands together and makes a strangled squeak like she's suppressing another excited squeal. Or at least trying to. I narrow my eyes at her before typing out a response.

> MELANIE
>
> Hey, West. Tomorrow morning would work.

> WEST
>
> Great! I know a place downtown. Can I pick you up?

> MELANIE
>
> That's okay, text me the address and time and I'll meet you there.

> WEST
>
> Alright. See you tomorrow.

"Why tomorrow and not today?" Noel asks, looking confused.

"Besides the fact that I need a day to emotionally prepare myself?" I scoff.

She bumps my hip with hers. "You're so dramatic."

"Actually, I'm going to swim laps today. I used to go all the time and want to start again."

"That's a great idea!"

I grin. "You wanna come with me?"

She backs away from me slowly. "No thanks, I prefer to exercise my mind. But you have fun!"

I creep towards her. "You know you want to."

Noel turns and runs toward her bedroom, yelling, "I have papers to grade!" Her door closes.

I chuckle to myself at how ridiculous she is, then head back to my room to find my old swimsuit.

———

I flail around in the freezing cold water, trying desperately to get above the layer of ice so I can breathe. The sunlight beams through the ice but offers no warmth to my freezing skin.

This is it. This is when my life ends. Doing something simple like ice skating with my dad and brother.

I'm getting tired, about to give up, when I hear Harrison's voice. I follow the sound and finally find the hole I fell through. I come up gasping for air.

My limbs feel limp, but I have to keep clinging to the edge of the ice. Harrison is laying on the ice, holding my hand. His voice is starting to fade as he encourages me to keep calm until Dad can get help. I'm so cold now, I can't feel my body, and my mind is fuzzy. The sky is starting to get dark so I'm hoping Dad gets help soon.

I wake up in a panic, my body drenched with sweat. My breaths are coming quickly like I just ran sprints. Glancing at my phone, I see it's barely six am. All I want to do is cry, but I know that won't help. Instead, I jump out of bed and walk to my closet to re-organize it. It's already in color order... but I can change it to brand names. In alphabetical order, of course.

I spend two hours organizing my already organized closet and I'm still rattled from the familiar nightmare. But I've calmed down enough that I'm no longer shaking. My stomach has settled too, which is good, since I'm already nervous enough about my coffee date with West.

Not date... meeting. Coffee meeting.

Moving from my closet to the bathroom, I start getting ready. First, I apply my best "no makeup" makeup look. I want to look amazing but not like I'm trying too hard. Basically, I'm shooting for effortlessly amazing. Next, I walk back to my immaculate closet to get dressed. After trying on what feels like one-hundred different outfits, my closet is completely disheveled. What a waste of impeccable organizing skills. Clothes cover every surface in my small bedroom... except my body, and I need to leave in ten minutes. So much for the two hours of organizing I did.

Noel knocks on my door and I walk through the mess to open it.

She glances around my normally pristine room with a horrified expression. "Um, you need some help picking an outfit?"

I turn and flop onto my bed with a groan. "Yes."

She claps a few times. "Get up! We have work to do. Where are your black jeans?"

I stand and rummage through the pile on my bed to find them.

"Okay, put these on. They make your butt look good."

She puts her hands on her hips and bites her bottom lip as she ponders her next idea. "Now, how about a white tee?" She spots one on the bed before I do and grabs it.

I pull on the jeans and then the tee while Noel continues rummaging. She selects my light denim jacket, white converse sneakers, and small stud earrings.

Once I've gotten dressed in the items she chose, I look in my floor-length mirror next to my closet door. "Noel, this is my old One Direction T-shirt."

"Oh well, you don't have any time left to change. Just button up your jacket." She spins me toward the door and gives me a shove. "Now go have fun on your coffee date."

"Just coffee. Not a date."

"Okay, sure."

————

Half an hour later, I'm pulling up outside the cafe West told me to meet him at. Downtown is busy as usual with a steady hum of traffic, tires screeching, and the occasional honk. I'm stressed about finding a parking spot. Not knowing the parking situation always makes me a little panicky. The thought of possibly having to parallel park doesn't help either. This is why I take the metro all week, and rarely drive my car downtown.

I circle around the block with no luck. As I come back around, I see a spot right in front of the cafe. It's a great spot, but, of course, I have to parallel park. With a deep breath, I internally go through my driver's handbook. I pull up next to the car in front of the parking spot and begin backing into the empty space.

There are several people walking on the sidewalk near me, but they're not paying attention to me, thank goodness. A man moves forward from the bustle of passerby, catching my eye. It's West in all of his masculine glory, standing on the sidewalk watching me curiously. His hands are in his pockets and he's grinning.

It's at that moment that my competitive drive kicks in. I will parallel park as I've never parallel parked before. It will be seamless, effortless, otherworldly. West will be speechless after watching such amazing parallel parking skills.

Prepare to be amazed, Weston Kershaw. I've thrived without you these past five years. And I'll prove it by parking in this tight spot.

I continue to drive forward and backward what feels like fifty times before I'm finally parked. My little Toyota Corolla is way off center, but it's good enough. I can feel West's eyes on me, but I refuse to be embarrassed by my car being slightly crooked... okay *really* crooked.

Grabbing my purse, I turn to open my door, but West is right there and opens it for me.

"Good morning." One side of his mouth pulls up, he looks amused. Obviously entertained by my lack of parking skills.

I feel flustered by his closeness; I wasn't expecting him to open my door. "Hey. Sorry it took me so long to park."

He chuckles and points to a shiny red sports car across the street. "I didn't do any better."

His car is parked just as poorly as mine. I breathe a sigh of relief. I don't know why I even care. I just didn't want to look like a fool to him... again.

We start walking toward the cafe and he pulls a ball cap out of his worn jeans. He pulls it down over his shaggy blonde locks, then slides large sunglasses on over his eyes. I can't help but be a little disappointed that he's obstructing my view of his handsomeness.

He must have noticed the look on my face and explains, "I tend to be recognized... I don't want our conversation to be interrupted by people asking for photos."

I cross my arms. "A little cocky are we?"

Before he can answer, two girls who look to be in their teens approach us. "Excuse me," one of them says. "are you Weston Kershaw?"

His shoulders slump just enough for me to notice but he quickly disguises his annoyance and smiles at them. "Let's make a deal: You guys take a selfie with me, but don't tell anyone. I'm trying to stay incognito." He slides his sunglasses down and winks, making them giggle.

The girls take several selfies with West, then whisper their thanks. The girls titter off down the sidewalk, giggling and glancing over their shoulders at him.

West slides his sunglasses back up his nose and pops up

the collar of his jacket, like covering his beard-covered chin will make him unrecognizable.

"Does that happen a lot?" I ask as we reach the cafe.

He holds the door open with one hand and places the other at the small of my back. Even through my jacket, the feel of his large hand sends warmth and a shiver of delight through my body.

Play it cool, hormones.

"Yeah, it does. Sorry about that. I reserved a table in the back corner of the cafe so people won't notice me. I know how ridiculous that sounds." He tilts his head down and we get in line.

I look around the cafe. It's bustling with people. No one seems to notice West though, as they're either glued to their phones or enjoying conversations with friends. We manage to order and he guides me back to the corner table. The from of the cafe is mostly glass, so you can see the busy street. But toward the back it's darker, with taupe colored walls and brown accents, which gives it a warm and cozy vibe. The brown leather armchairs around the small round tables give the cafe an opulent look.

The table West requested is behind a short wall in the back, blocking us from the rest of the cafe. I understand why he requested this table, but being alone with him makes me nervous. He pulls my chair out for me then sits across from me.

"This place is so pretty, I haven't been here before."

"It's close to the Eagle's arena we use for practice, so me and the guys come here quite a bit." He places his forearms on the table and laces his fingers together.

There's a beat of silence between us, neither sure what to say next. The waitress stops by our table with our with West's black coffee and my chai tea. I'm grateful for the interruption so I can gather my wits.

"So, how do you like D.C. so far?" I ask once the waitress leaves.

He blows on his coffee to cool it down. "I really like it, actually. Canada's winters are so long. That was always something I hated about Minnesota too." He smirks and takes a sip of coffee.

"Really? I never realized the cold bothered you. I miss Minnesota winters." I smile to myself and pick up my mug. I can still remember the days spent bundled up playing in the snow. Usually with Harrison and West.

My eyes meet his over my mug. "There were definitely things I loved about Minnesota," He says without looking away, his eyes searing into mine.

The way he said it sounded almost flirtatious, but why would West be flirting with me after all these years?

I look down at my mug and take another sip. "Like hanging out with Harrison?"

His face falls briefly before he smiles, but it looks forced. "Yeah, sure."

We stare at each other for a moment. I feel like I need to re-familiarize myself with this adult version of the boy I used to know. His face has lost some of its youthful chub, making his jaw and cheekbones more defined. Even his well-trimmed beard can't hide that jaw line. His hair is still shaggy but shorter than he had it in high school. And there's a tuft of light brown chest hair peeking out the top of his v-neck tee.

He smirks at my obvious perusal. "So, you're still a Directioner, huh?" His eyes glance down at my T-shirt.

I close my eyes, feeling embarrassed. I completely forgot to button up my jacket. "Ha. I mean, they're timeless." I attempt a casual shrug.

He laughs and it sounds more deep and husky than I remember. I'm unable to stop the smile that spreads across my face. I always loved his laugh. Being here with him feels surprisingly normal, which makes me feel silly that we've tiptoed around each other all these years. "Do you enjoy your job? The congressman seems nice, Madden is his name?" West asks before sliding his jacket off and hanging it on the back of his chair.

"I love my job." I smile and remove my jacket as well; he's already seen my One Direction shirt, and the tea is making me hot. That, and the incessant blush that takes residence on my face anytime I'm near West. "Working for Madden has given me a lot of experience in assisting, and his wife is super sweet too. If he doesn't run for Congress again, I hope to find another similar position."

West nods. "You always were great at organization. Pretty sure It's thanks to you Harrison and I made it on time to practice most days. And remembered all of our gear."

I take another sip of my tea. "Uh, yeah. You guys really owe me. I even used to unload your bags after hockey practices to let your gear air out so you wouldn't smell putrid."

He's taking a drink of coffee but huffs a laugh out through his nose. "You're not wrong. I should probably send my next paycheck straight to you."

"Just hire me as your live-in assistant if anything happens to my current job," I say before clamping my mouth shut. I meant it sarcastically, but it sounded more like flirting.

A slow grin spreads across his face. "That could be arranged."

He slowly brings his mug to his lips and takes a long sip, his eyes gazing into mine the whole time. The hairs on my neck raise just by the look he's giving me. When we were teenagers, I felt like there was an attraction between us, but he's never looked at me quite like this. His heated gaze gives me the impression he wants to devour me. It's hard to think when he looks at me like that.

"Weston!" A woman's voice comes from behind me, her voice is heavily accented making Weston sound more like *Veston*.

West's eyes fly wide open. I turn in my seat and look at the woman. She's stunning. Probably six feet tall, long legs that were made for walking a runway, and dark hair that falls down to her waist. She's beautiful, angry, and also a little terrifying.

"Who is this?!" She yells, pointing to me indignantly.

My head whips back and forth between West and the angry lady.

West finally comes out of his stunned silence. "Katarina? What are you doing here?"

Her lips twist in annoyance. "You said we couldn't be together because you were moving to the capital city." Her arm bends and she places a fist on her slender hip. "So I moved too."

West's elbows are resting on the table in front of us and he brings his hands up to cradle his face before dragging them through his hair. "You didn't seriously move here, did you?"

"Of course!" She whips her long hair over her shoulder, drawing attention to her defined collar bones and long neck. "We belong together, Weston."

I have to pay close attention when she's speaking because her accent is so strong, I'm guessing it's Russian, or Ukrainian? I feel very uncomfortable being here in the middle of what should be a private conversation. I was such a moron to think West was sitting here flirting with me when these are the type of women he dates.

Don't get me wrong; I don't think I'm ugly. I'm cute, I have great curves, I like the way I look. But I'm no Katarina. I rise from my seat and pull out a few dollars to leave for a tip and set it on the table.

"I'll give you two some privacy."

West shoots up from his chair. "Melanie, please stay." He looks at Katarina. "You need to leave, Kat. Can't we talk about this later?"

When he calls her *Kat*, an unwanted pang of jealousy shoots through me. That little endearment tells me they meant something to each other at one point.

Katarina looks down at me. "Actually, *you* may leave, tiny person."

She smirks before walking over to West's side and grabbing onto his hand, he tries to pull away but her other hand goes to his bicep and she sinks her claws into him, literally. Her fingernails are long and pointy. I seriously hope she doesn't puncture his skin with those things.

West turns to face her. "No, *you're* leaving. She's staying."

CHAPTER
SEVEN
WEST

I QUICKLY REMOVE Kat's hand from my arm and take a step away from her so I'm side by side with Mel. We're so close, our arms brush briefly, sending a jolt of warmth and awareness through me. Melanie stills and looks up at me, two pink dots color her cheeks, making me think she felt the same rush of heat that I did.

Kat huffs a snide laugh and we both snap our heads to look at her. She gestures toward Melanie with one perfectly manicured hand. "Don't tell me you're on a date with this... what's the English word... peasant?" She spits the word *peasant* like it's a curse.

Before my brain registers what my body is doing, my arm wraps around Mel's waist, pulling her into my side. "Actually, this stunning and intelligent woman is, in fact, my girlfriend."

Wait, what? Did I just say that out loud?

Melanie's head whips over to look at me, her eyes wide with surprise, and maybe a hint of annoyance. *Oops.*

I lift my eyebrows and shift my eyes to Kat a few times, silently begging Mel to play along. She releases a small sigh and relaxes again. Mel slides her hand through my arm, her hand is now resting on my bicep. The warmth of her hand on my skin soothes something deep inside me. It's the comfort of being with a childhood friend, but mixed with the heat of attraction. It feels good. Perfect, actually.

A sinister laugh bubbles out of Katarina before she says, "I don't believe it for a second. He's completely out of your league, *child*."

Melanie tenses next to me. I can't believe I actually dated Katarina. Could I really not see how mean-spirited she is?

I clench my jaw. "Don't ever talk to Mel like that."

Kat crosses her arms and pops a hip out. "Fine. But I'm not leaving until you prove to me this woman is your girlfriend," she says in a challenge, her eyes drilling into mine.

My mind briefly registers that Katarina's drama is starting to draw a crowd, people throughout the cafe are craning their necks to see what's going on. But does that stop me from doing what I do next? Nope.

I turn toward Melanie and wrap my arms around her waist, pulling her close so her chest is pressed against mine. She fits me like no one ever has before. Her eyes blink rapidly, at my sudden movement but she doesn't push me away.

Gently, I use my free hand to tilt her chin up, then I plant a kiss right on her gorgeous, pillowy-soft lips.

She's stiff for a second, probably confused by my actions. But then she tilts her head to the side, giving our kiss a better angle. To my surprise, her hands grab ahold of my biceps and we kiss each other like it's just the two of us here in this cafe. But then the patrons in said cafe begin to clap and whistle.

We jump apart to see dozens of people recording and taking photos with their phones.

Kat's mouth is wide open, gaping at us. She makes a noise that sounds like a growl and a huff of annoyance mixed together. She spins on her heel and stomps toward the door to leave. When she's in the middle of the cafe, she turns back and narrows her eyes at Melanie and says, "Enjoy it while it lasts. Soon he'll be tired of you and he'll come crawling back to me."

And with that, she stomps out the door of the cafe. The people surrounding us are getting closer and asking for photos and autographs. I can tell by Melanie's pale face and wide eyes that she's getting overwhelmed. Wrapping my arms around her shoulders, I guide her out of the cafe and to my car.

Once we're both inside the vehicle, I start driving, wanting to get as far away from the crowd as I can. And allow Mel time to calm down.

We've been in the car for five minutes and she still hasn't uttered a word.

"I'm so sorry about that, Mel," I say, breaking the silence.

My eyes are on the road, but I hear her inhale a deep breath and blow it out slowly. "What the heck happened back there?"

"I broke up with Kat months ago—"

She interrupts me mid-sentence. "Not that. I mean the kiss."

"Oh." I can't help the smile tugging on the corners of my mouth thinking back to our kiss. "It was a pretty great kiss."

She groans. "West, why did you kiss me?"

"Well… she asked for proof you were my girlfriend so I kissed you."

Melanie's familiar scent of lavender and jasmine has filled the small cab of my car and I find myself momentarily savoring the fragrance. Kat, and most of the women I've dated, always wore strong perfumes that smelled artificial. In my opinion, women smell best fresh out of the shower, when they haven't spritzed any perfume on, sprayed on hairspray, or powdered their faces with makeup. Just the scent of their skin and shampoo… and maybe a few essential oils.

Admittedly, I haven't smelled many women freshly showered, but the memory of spending evenings at Harrison and Mel's house, when Melanie had just showered and thrown on some pajama pants and a T-shirt... perfection.

"But I'm *not* your girlfriend!" Melanie says, throwing her hands up in defeat. "You can't just go around kissing people you're not in a relationship with."

I keep one hand on the steering wheel and drag the other through my hair. "You're right, I'm sorry. It's just, Kat has serious stalker tendencies, and I freaked out."

Also, that was the best kiss of my life, and I want to repeat it—is what I'm thinking—but I'm not a big enough idiot to say it out loud. At least, not right now.

She sighs. "Listen, I don't want to drudge up the past, but I was really hurt when you stopped talking to me after that stupid video. And you can't just pull a 180 on me, calling me up to hang out with me, or kissing me when it's convenient for you."

My chest feels tight; I hate that I hurt her again. "You're right, and I'm sorry for putting you in that position."

"It's okay. I mean, I willingly went along with it... so it's not all on you." I can hear the smile in her voice, which puts me at ease. "I really would like for us to be friends again, though. If you're up for it."

I turn my head to look at her, considering her words. I'd like to be more than just friends. Actually, I'd like to kiss her again, and smell her when she's fresh out of the shower. But I don't have a death wish, so I answer with, "I'd like that."

We smile at each other, causing me to nearly rear-end the vehicle in front of me.

Freaking D.C. traffic.

———

After dropping Melanie off at her vehicle, I head to hockey practice. I barely made it on time thanks to the ruckus Kat caused.

When I walk into the locker room all of the other guys stop what they're doing and begin to applaud. My brow furrows in confusion.

Huffing out a small laugh, I ask, "What's this all about?"

Our team captain, Ford Remington, or Remy as we call him, is the only one not taking part in the teasing. He rolls his eyes before turning his back to the room. He's the oldest one on the team at a whopping thirty-three-years old, and definitely the most mature.

"Your lady friend stopped by looking for you," Colby Knight is the first to speak up. I take a seat next to him on our bench.

Mitch Anderson scoffs from my other direction. "I'll never understand how you get all these beautiful women fawning all over you."

I ignore him and turn my head to speak to Colby. "Who was it?"

"She was super tall, moved like a gazelle, and had an accent." He smirks and leans in to whisper, "She was also a little terrifying."

I run a hand down my face. "Katarina? She came *here*? Ugh."

"Yeah, man. The guys have been in an uproar about having a model come to the rink. Mitch told her you always visit the Patriot Cafe before practice."

Whipping my head in my other direction, I glare at Mitch. This explains how Kat found me. "Why would you give out information like that? You know the crazy people we have to deal with!"

He shoots me a sardonic smile and I grit my teeth together

to keep myself from saying something I'll regret. Remy must've overheard the conversation and takes a few steps across the room in our direction.

He frowns at Mitch. "We don't give out personal information about our teammates, or *anyone* working for the Eagles. I don't care if it's Coach Young or an intern. Are we understood?"

Mitch squares his shoulders and clenches his jaw. "Yeah, Remington. I got it."

Once we're all suited up, we split off into teams for practice. As soon as I'm on the ice, the stress of this morning begins to melt away. I breathe the cold air into my lungs as I skate a few laps to warm up. Even the sound of my skates hitting the ice calms me. The ice is where I decompress, and also where I work out any frustrations.

There's a reason they say if you can't play nice, play hockey. And there's a certain teammate who's going to learn what happens when his actions affect the people I love.

Now that we're all warmed up, coach drops the puck and I face off against Mitch. I take possession of the puck and take it out of the neutral zone, leaving Mitch snarling in my wake. I pass the puck to Remy, and he skates it closer to the net before passing it to Colby. Mitch is skating over to block Colby's shot, but I get to him first and body check him. Upon impact, he groans and falls on his back, sliding a few feet on the ice before stopping.

He gets up quickly and his lip curls in a snarl. "What was that for?" He yells.

"It was a clean hit." I shrug.

Mitch flies at me and grabs my jersey. He draws his arm back to punch me, but coach skates over and gets between us before his fist meets my jaw.

"You two need to cool it!" Coach Young places a palm on

each of our chests to keep us apart. "This is just practice, boys. Remember you're normally on the *same* team."

Mitch's face is still twisted in anger like he wants to brawl. And honestly, I'd welcome the chance to get a few more hits in.

"Pretty sure West is the one needing reminded of that." Mitch sneers.

"Says the guy who gave my personal whereabouts to a stranger," I snap back.

"Both of you shut up!" Coach demands before dragging his hand down his face in frustration. "This isn't daycare, and I'm not a babysitter. So pull up your big boy underwear and deal with your personal issues later." He narrows his eyes at me and Mitch before skating back off the ice.

We continue our game, but glare at each other for the rest of practice.

I avoid Mitch afterward in the showers and locker room, but when I walk outside to my car, he's leaning against it.

"What's your problem?" Mitch asks when I'm within earshot.

"*My* problem?" I pin him with a serious expression. "Teammates are supposed to have each other's backs. But you're over here buddying up to my certifiably insane exes."

"I thought she was your girlfriend. That's how she made it sound." He shrugs unapologetically.

"I'm not even worried about myself here, but your actions caused unnecessary drama and hurt someone I love."

He huffs out a laugh. "Okay, I shouldn't have told her where you were. But you're blowing this out of proportion."

"Am I?"

"I know your kind, golden boy. Guys like you who've been handed everything in life can't seem to let the small things just roll off of their shoulders." He removes himself from my car and starts to walk away.

I cock my head and look at him in confusion. "What are you talking about?"

"You waltz in here like you own the place, slapping on assistant captain right away." He scoffs. "When some of us have been busting our asses on this team for *years* only to be completely overlooked."

I'm silent as he stalks over to his vehicle, gets inside, and drives off.

"Don't worry about Mitch."

I look over my shoulder to see Colby Knight walking toward me. He continues speaking, "He had a pretty rough upbringing, dad's in jail. I don't know all the details." He shrugs. "But he's the best defenseman we have. One of the best in the league in my opinion."

"That explains a lot." I blow out a breath. "But still, the guys a jerk."

"He's prickly, but you'll learn to love him... eventually." He smirks.

I huff out an unconvinced laugh. "Anyway. Wanna grab some dinner?"

"You buying, Mr. Hotshot Assistant Captain?" He asks with a grin.

"Fine." I gesture to my car. "Hop in."

CHAPTER
EIGHT

MELANIE

NOEL SITS on the sofa next to me with a stunned expression on her face. I just rehashed all the details of the drama that happened at the cafe this morning. Noel, of course, listened in rapt attention.

"So, he just grabbed you and kissed you?!"

"Yep. And don't get me wrong, the man can kiss. Oh my, can he kiss." I sigh. "I don't know how he managed to charm my defenses away so fast."

She rests one elbow on the back of the couch and turns to look at me. "That's some hot caveman stuff right there, Mel. He's gotta have feelings for you. Guys don't just randomly kiss people to get rid of their exes."

"If it wouldn't have been for Katarina stopping by, I think I'd agree with you. I mean, it definitely felt like he was flirting." I purse my lips. "But Katarina was flawlessly stunning. I'm sure they were the picture-perfect couple. Their children would've been gorgeous freaks of nature."

Her mouth twists in annoyance. "So?"

"Remember the other night when we scrolled through Google images of West? Every woman with him in those photos was tall, model-thin, and gorgeous." Noel opens her mouth to talk but I put my hand up to stop her so I can explain myself better. "Don't get me wrong, I don't think I'm a troll or anything. But I'm pretty sure I'm not West's *type*."

Noel turns to face me and crosses her arms. She looks irritated. "Do you see him happily in a long-term relationship with any of those models?"

Before I can respond, she continues, "Yeah. Exactly. Plus, what if someone thought Jeff was *your* type?" She raises one eyebrow like she's challenging me to disagree. "Then every boring man in the county would be knocking on your door."

I roll my eyes. "Jeff wasn't *that* boring. But I get your point."

"Good." She shoots me a smug grin. "People can be attracted to all different types. For example, Aragorn from *Lord of the Rings* is extremely sexy because he's so rugged and manly. But Legolas is equally as hot because he's got that whole beautiful elf thing going on."

I laugh. "You're so strange."

"It's part of my charm." She shrugs.

A notification chimes on Noel's phone and she takes it out of her hoodie pocket, a hoodie that says *the best boyfriends are fictional*, and looks at the screen. She grimaces and turns to me, facing her phone screen so I can see it.

I look at the screen, confused for a few seconds. It's a photo —actually a myriad of photos—of Katarina, West, and myself at the cafe this morning. In the first few, it just looks like the three of us are chatting, but as we scroll through, there are photos of him wrapping his arm around my waist, and then more of him kissing me.

"Oh no. This cannot be happening." I groan and thread my hands into my hair. "Wait, do you have Google notifications on for West?"

She ducks her chin, knowing she's been found out. "Um, yeah. Just wanted to keep tabs on the situation." She leans forward and studies the photos. "Girl, that kiss looks hot."

She puts her phone right in my face and I shove it away. "Don't make this a thing."

Noel laughs. "Mel, this is already a thing. It's all over the internet. There's even a trending hashtag... #KissinKershaw."

My eyes widen with panic. "Noel! My boss is going to see these!"

She grimaces. "Probably."

I gasp. "And my brother!"

She nods and puts an arm around my shoulder. "It'll be okay. You're a young, single woman. Sometimes you're going to get caught sucking face with famous hockey players."

"You make it sound like this happens to all twenty-three year olds."

She chuckles. "If it makes you feel any better, when I was your age, I was dressing up like Hermoine from Harry Potter for Comic-Con. And other nerdy things. Nothing as awesome as sharing hot kisses with yummy guys."

I try to hold back my laugh, but it's impossible. "You're only two years older than me, you know? And I love that you're a huge nerd." I rest my head on her shoulder. "But thanks for making me feel a little better."

"Anytime, girl."

CHAPTER
NINE
WEST

THE MOMENT I walk through my front door after arriving home from dinner with Colby, my phone rings. Slipping my shoes off on the front mat, I pull my phone out of my jeans pocket. It's Harrison.

I let my head drop back and look at the ceiling in agony. All I want to do is relax and wind down. But I know I have to answer. I can only assume the pictures people took at the cafe have hit the internet by now. It never takes long.

With a deep, steadying breath, I answer, "Hey, Harrison."

"Care to explain to me why there's a billion photos featuring you making out with my little sister?" He grits out the last part. He's most likely clenching his teeth like he always does when he's angry.

"We were not making out, it was just a peck."

He scoffs. "Didn't look like a peck from the photos!"

I walk into my kitchen, grab a water glass from the cabinet and fill it up while I explain to Harrison what happened with Katarina and how Melanie pretended to be my girlfriend.

"Okay, but nothing in that story indicates a reason for you

to kiss my sister," He says matter-of-factly. But his voice does sound more calm now. Whew.

I lean against the countertop and sigh. "You're right. I didn't *have* to kiss her, and I apologized to her about that." I roll my lips together before adding, "But… if I'm being completely honest, I've had feelings for Mel for a long time, and when I saw an opportunity to kiss her… I took it."

"Excuse me?" Harrison's voice is getting angry again. "Did you forget about a certain pact??"

"You can't be serious, Harrison. We made that pact when we were thirteen!" My free hand flies up in the air in aggravation, even though no one is here to see it.

I can picture the tic in his jaw that's probably happening right now. I bet his nostrils are also flared.

"*I've* kept our pact."

I snort a laugh through my nose. "My sisters are older than you and would never even be interested, and you know it." I take a bite of my sandwich to appease my stomach.

His heavy exhale sounds fuzzy through the phone. "Alright, forget about the pact. I'm more worried about the revolving door of women you've dated. Melanie isn't someone you can just have a fling with."

My shoulders slump, knowing he has a point. I definitely haven't made myself appear to be a serious relationship kind of guy. "I understand you wanting to protect her, and why you're worried. But I'd never hurt Melanie. I haven't even dated anyone since Kat, and I ended things with her before I even moved here."

"You're like a brother to me, West." He pauses for a second like he's contemplating his words. "But if you ever hurt Melanie, I will never forgive you."

I nod my head. "If I ever hurt Mel, I'd never forgive myself. But she's *it* for me, man. She always has been."

"So, are you going to like… date my sister?" His voice sounds annoyed, but at least he's not angry. I think.

"I'd really like to, if she'll let me. As far as I'm concerned, I've wasted the last five years *not* being with her." I rub the back of my neck. "But I have some work to do to win her over."

"Good, she should make you work for it."

I laugh but Harrison doesn't join me.

"Break her heart and I'll break your nose. I don't give a puck how famous your pretty face is." His voice sounds slightly more light-hearted now, but I know he's completely serious.

"You know I hate your hockey puns. But it's a deal."

————

It's Monday morning and I want to do something nice for Melanie. I'm sure she's at work being her responsible little self, but I bet Madden Windell's office wouldn't be too hard to find. I have some time before I need to leave for practice, so I do a quick Google search. Unfortunately, his address isn't listed anywhere, except for a post office box. It seems dramatic to send a letter to a congressman; there has to be another way to find his office so I can surprise her with something.

When I walk into the rink for practice an hour later, I notice Coach Young is in Tom's office. A thought pops into my head… Tom might have Madden Windell's contact information. I stop in my tracks and knock on the door frame.

Tom stands to his full height, which is almost as tall as I am. "Hey, West! Come on in," he says in his jovial voice.

His dark hair is cut short in a businessy style, which makes him stand out from the guys on the team. We tend to be a little more unkempt. Looking between him and Coach Young, I observe that they're both wearing their blue Eagles polos with black dress pants.

Coach Young must notice my amused expression and rolls his eyes. "Yes, we know we're matching again. And no, we didn't plan it."

Tom laughs; there's always a twinkle in his blue eyes like he's withholding a joke. "I'm going to start packing extra clothes, Coach. Then we won't have this issue."

One side of Coach's mouth pulls up slightly. "That's probably a good plan. We all know I'm better looking, and it's way more noticeable when we wear the same thing."

Tom scoffs and they start flexing their arms and laughing. It's nice to see Coach Young like this, having fun and joking around. He's always so serious with the guys on the team, but I suppose we give him more respect that way.

"Sorry, West. What did you need?" Tom asks, pulling his shirt sleeves back down after his impromptu gun show.

I clear my throat. "Actually, I was wondering if you happen to know the address of Madden Windell's office?"

Coach Young and Tom eye me curiously. Tom speaks again, "I don't, but I have his cell number. What do you need it for?"

I rub the back of my head with one hand. "Well, I wanted to send something to his assistant, Melanie."

Coach and Tom give each other a quick glance. Both of them are smirking.

"Ahh… of course it's about a girl. I'll let you handle this, Tom. I need to get to the locker room and keep the guys in line anyway." He slaps Tom on the shoulder and nods his head in my direction before leaving.

We listen for a moment until his steps are no longer echoing in the hallway. Tom crosses his arms over his chest and sits on the edge of his desk. "So the assistant, huh?"

"Yeah, we go way back actually."

"Oh, that's right." He nods. "You're good friends with her brother?"

"Harrison. He's my best friend," I tell him.

He crosses his feet at his ankles. "So, since you go way back, shouldn't you already know where she works?"

I sigh. "We kind of lost touch for a while."

He grins. "So you want to woo her?" He raises his eyebrows up and down a few times, making me laugh.

"Basically, yes."

"I'll give you Madden's number and his office address, but promise me one thing."

"Alright," I answer quickly, knowing Tom wouldn't ask something ridiculous of me. At least, I don't think he would.

"Don't send her a signed jersey. Trust me, that's not the way to romance a woman." He pins me with a serious gaze.

I scoff. "I'd never do that; I'm not a complete moron." I *had* actually thought about doing that, so I'm thankful for this piece of advice.

He breathes a sigh of relief and laughs. "Thank goodness. I'll text you the information right away."

"Thanks, man, I appreciate it."

CHAPTER
TEN
MELANIE

MONDAY AFTERNOON, I walk into the office after my lunch break. Madden is traveling home to Kansas on Friday for a few weeks. We have a lot to get done this week before he leaves.

I open the door to the office space Madden rents in this building and my heels clack against the tile as I walk toward my desk. The office decor is sleek and modern, so the grandiose flower arrangement on my desk stands out like someone in Minnesota who doesn't know how to ice skate.

I stop a few paces before my desk and stare at the exquisite arrangement. Madden appears in the doorway of his office and leans against the doorframe. He has a smirk on his face and looks from me to the fragrant bouquet. Upon first glance, the bouquet is full of lavender and jasmine flowers, but there are also white roses throughout. It smells incredible and is huge, taking up most of my desk. I blink a few times and look from the flowers back to Madden.

He clears his throat, still smirking. "You received a delivery while you were at lunch."

"Are you sure these are for me?" I ask, staring at the extravagant arrangement.

"Well, they're definitely not for me." He chuckles.

I step forward and find a little card peeking out of the flowers. The card just says *Mel*. Madden grins at me and ducks back into his office. I rip the envelope open and read it.

I'm so sorry about our coffee date being interrupted. You mean so much to me and I hate that we've grown apart. Please have dinner with me tonight?
-West

A strange mixture of emotions swirl through me: tears in my eyes because he's missed me, nervous energy making my hands shake at him telling me how much I mean to him, and flutters in my stomach at the thought of having dinner with him. This many emotions at once is so overwhelming, I take a seat in my white leather swivel chair because I feel a little light-headed. I grab a tissue from my desk and dab at my eyes.

With a deep breath, I pull my phone out of my purse and type out a text.

MEL

Thank you for the beautiful flowers.

Biting my bottom lip, I think about his having dinner with him. My heart wants to, by my head is telling me to be cautious. But would it really hurt just to have dinner with him?

MEL

What time are you thinking for dinner?

I'm so weak, I know. Setting my phone down on my lap, I close my eyes. My hands are shaking from my nervous energy. I jump when my phone pings, and I quickly look down at the screen.

WEST

How about 7 pm?

MEL

Sounds good.

He sends me a Google Maps link to an address. It's in a ritzy part of town and looks like a residential address. Interesting.

The rest of the workday drags by—probably because I check the time every five minutes. I'll have to leave straight from work to meet West tonight, so I'm happy I look my best today. Grey pin-striped pencil skirt with a pink, fitted bodysuit underneath. My hair is freshly washed and blown out, so my curtain bangs and layers are extra bouncy. I even took a little longer on my makeup today to make myself feel better. When you look good you feel good, right?

I finish up responding to some emails for Madden, and then it's finally time to leave. Tidying up my desk, I make sure my pens are in alphabetical order by color (which is so helpful when you're in a rush). After plugging my work iPad in, I grab my mini dust vacuum and clean up my area. I also have cute pink drawer organizers for everything and I like to make sure it's perfect for when I arrive in the morning for a new day.

I do this same routine before I leave work each day… and if I forget, I can hardly sleep that night. I learned this the hard way.

With a satisfied sigh, I stand and smooth my skirt before

peeking into Madden's office. He's sitting behind his large desk and looks up when I clear my throat.

"Hey, I'm heading out. See you tomorrow." I smile and he smiles back.

"Sounds good, thanks, Melanie!" He gives me a little salute.

I make it down to the metro and find the line I need to get to the address West sent me. It's 6:30 now, so I should arrive just a few minutes after seven. I hate being late, but I'm sure he'll understand since I was at work.

During the thirty-minute ride I check my schedule for tomorrow and make sure I added all of Madden's appointments to his calendar. Before I know it, I'm at my stop and pull up the address West sent me again. Thankfully, it's just a few blocks from the metro since I'm wearing heels and all.

I follow the address and am surprised when I arrive in front of a gorgeous townhouse. It looks to be three stories high, with a bay window on each level. It's a light grey, almost white, color and has brick steps leading up to a black door with gold hardware. The townhomes surrounding it are just as beautiful and the lawns are well-manicured.

Is this West's house? I check the address to make sure I'm at the correct place. Yep, this is definitely the correct address.

I walk to the front door and bring my hand up to knock, but West opens it before my fist hits the door. He has a grin on his face, and his hair looks slightly damp like he recently showered. He's wearing dark jeans with a flannel button-up shirt and his feet are bare. I feel my cheeks heat. What is it about bare feet and damp hair that feels so intimate?

"Hey Mel, you look beautiful." His eyes roam from my feet to my eyes, but not in a suggestive way. Just him taking me in as I did to him.

My cheeks feel even warmer at his compliment. "Thank you."

"Come on in." He moves to the side and holds the door open for me.

I step inside and my eyes widen. I knew West would live in a nice place; I mean, he's a multimillionaire and everything. But this place is so cozy and warm, not like the bachelor pad with sharp lines I would imagine a professional athlete would have. The walls on the right are all exposed brick, and the walls on the left are hunter green. There's a tufted, cognac-leather couch and two matching armchairs in the living area, and instead of a TV, there's just a fireplace and some family photos displayed. The space is large and open so I can see the dining and kitchen from where I'm standing. The kitchen cabinets are a dusty blue color with modern gold hardware that matches the front door. White marble countertops and stainless steel appliances complete the look.

"Wow, West. This is gorgeous. I'm assuming this is *your* house?"

He laughs. "Yes, this is my place. And thank you."

I walk over to the fireplace to look at the framed photos on the mantle. I notice there are several large dark blue stones placed around the photos, and I wonder if he chose them or if a designer put them there.

Glancing over my shoulder, I say, "I was expecting to meet you at a restaurant or something."

He shrugs. "This is more private. Less fans asking for photos."

I nod and turn back toward the photos. Most of them are of West and his parents along with his two older sisters. There's also one of him ice skating with his nephews and another of him and Harrison from college. Then there's one of me, West, and Harrison from their senior year of high school. It's prom and we're all dressed up. I notice West has his arm around my waist and I'm leaning into him, Harrison looks like a third wheel standing about a foot away from us. We're all smiling at the camera.

"I considered cutting Harrison out of that one, but I knew he'd whine about it." West says from behind me with a chuckle.

I turn to look at him and smirk, knowing he's right. "I can't believe you still have this picture. I haven't seen it in years."

His face turns serious. "Just because we haven't *really* talked in years doesn't mean I forgot about you."

I gulp, the air between us feeling suddenly heavy with an emotion I can't explain. Memories, attraction, regret. Perhaps all three?

He takes a step back, putting some space between us. "Listen, I just need you to know that I broke up with Katarina months ago, before I even moved." He purses his lips and drags a hand down his face. "The tabloids make it sound like I move from woman to woman every week, and that's not accurate."

"Okay… It must suck constantly being in the public eye."

"It's not always fun." He smiles. "I've dated, obviously, but I don't even have time to take out a different girl every week. Even if I wanted to." He huffs a laugh. "Which I don't," He adds the last part with wide eyes like he was concerned I'd think otherwise.

I chuckle. "I believe you."

His shoulders relax. "So, anyway. Dinner is ready. Are you hungry?"

"I am, actually. Did you cook?" I quirk an eyebrow. I can't remember West ever cooking.

He laughs. "I did. Hopefully it turned out okay. I took some cooking lessons in Canada for fun. I got tired of takeout." He sticks his hands in his pockets, making him look like the boy I knew all those years ago.

"I'm sure it'll be great. Anything homemade is a treat."

He gestures toward the round dining table. The wood looks fashionably distressed and it's surrounded by matching upholstered chairs. The table is set for two and he pulls my chair out for me before walking into the kitchen and taking a tray out of the oven.

West plates the food then picks up a tablet from the kitchen counter, taps the screen a few times, and music begins playing softly throughout the room. The music is upbeat and French, I believe it's Carla Bruni.

He smiles at me from the kitchen and I laugh. "Wow, you're so fancy now. Listening to French music."

He laughs, it's the laugh I remember from my childhood. He's not holding back or trying to impress anyone, just his normal, goofy laugh. It warms my heart.

"I'm just the same kid you grew up with. The only thing different is my bank account." He gives me an over-exaggerated wink and I giggle.

This feels normal and comfortable, which gives me hope we can fix this... whatever *this* is, happening between us.

I cut into my baked chicken. "There are definitely a few things that have changed besides your income," I say before taking a bite. The breaded chicken is savory and delicious.

He quirks his head to the side. "Really? Like what?"

I swallow and take a sip of water. "For starters, you have chest hair now." I snicker.

He looks down at the patch of hair peeking out at the top of his shirt. He grins and glances up at me, his eyes twinkling with mischief. "I can't believe you've been staring at my chest, I'm more than just hot bod, you know."

My jaw drops slightly before I notice one corner of his

mouth turning up, like he's suppressing a laugh. I playfully slap him on the shoulder, and wow, a very firm and muscular shoulder it is.

"You're so full of yourself," I say with a laugh.

His head falls back as he laughs, cracking himself up just like he did back in high school. "I'm sorry, I couldn't resist." West rubs the scruff on his jaw. "I can finally grow facial hair now, too."

"I noticed. It looks good." I blush, regretting being so forthcoming.

"Thanks," West says with a smile. "I was always jealous of Harrison's ability to grow a beard."

I laugh. "So, what about me? Have I changed at all?"

A blush appears on his cheeks and neck. It's barely noticeable with his tanned skin and short beard. He huffs out a laugh. "Um, yeah."

He shoves a large bite of chicken in his mouth as if that'll keep him from having to answer the question.

I purse my lips, annoyed he didn't expound on that. "Like how?" I ask.

He points to his mouth, which is full of food, and widens his eyes as if to say he can't answer because his mouth is full.

I cross my arms and lean back in my chair, waiting for him to finish. I check my wrist even though I'm not wearing a watch, just to let him know I'm awaiting his answer.

He swallows and takes a drink of his water. He keeps drinking until he's nearly finished the entire glass.

I roll my eyes. "Oh my gosh. Just answer the question already! I answered yours."

He takes a deep breath and blows it out slowly. "Alright. Well…" He clears his throat. "You've always been beautiful, Mel. But like a princess in a story book, with your big blue eyes and all." He finishes his water before continuing. "But now you're a beautiful *woman*. You've transformed into a confident, strong queen. Nothing princess-like about you anymore."

His gaze doesn't stray from mine as he says it. There's no hint of humor in his voice now. I feel my cheeks heating again —actually, my entire body suddenly feels hot.

"Oh, thank you." I take a drink of my cold water to cool myself down.

CHAPTER
ELEVEN
WEST

SITTING NEXT TO MELANIE, in my house, looking into her eyes... it makes me feel like I've just been sleepwalking for the last five years and I've finally woken up. More awake than hockey makes me feel, or even winning a game. I can't fathom that I ever thought my feelings for her would just go away, that I could find someone who made me feel the same way she does. That my feelings for her were just some silly teenage crush.

I wasn't lying when I told her she'd changed from a girl to a woman, from a princess to a queen... but her gorgeous blue eyes *are* still the same. Their deep blue color has always captivated me. My eyes are so light blue they're almost grey. But Melanie's large, round eyes are a dark azurite blue. Azurite has long been my favorite color, and I had convinced myself the azurite stones on my mantle were purely for decoration. But really, they just reminded me of her eyes.

We finish eating and I take our plates into the kitchen. Melanie follows with the water pitcher and glasses. "You don't have to get that, you're my guest," I say.

"I don't mind. You *did* make dinner after all. The least I can do is help clean up." She turns the faucet on and grabs the scrub brush and soap.

She looks determined so I don't argue. Plus, I know she genuinely loves cleaning and organizing. I help her by loading the smaller items into the dishwasher, and she starts washing the skillet I used tonight. It feels like we're an old married couple, and I don't hate it.

"So, Harrison is visiting next week?" I ask.

"Yeah! I'm excited to see him. With his work schedule, he only visits about once a year."

I lean against the counter. "I keep telling him I can get him a job with the Eagles. We could always use a good physical therapist."

"Oh, that would be amazing! He loves his job in Philly so much though, not sure he'll ever move." She shrugs but continues scrubbing the pan.

"Where does he stay when he visits?"

She wrinkles her nose. "He gets a hotel; my place is tiny. Just enough room for me and my roommate."

I grab a towel and begin drying the dishes she has washed. "You have a roommate?"

I shouldn't be surprised; D.C. is expensive, and she probably feels safer with a roommate. What if it's a guy? I'll kill him.

"Yeah!" She grins and hands me another dish. "Noel. We met at college. She was already working on her PhD, but we ran into each other in the library and hit it off."

Internally, I breathe a sigh of relief. "Very cool, I'll have to meet her sometime."

She smirks. "Alright, but you should know… she hates sports."

My eyebrows shoot up. "What? Why?"

"She's a history professor. One of those bookish academic

types." She chuckles to herself, like a funny memory just popped into her head. "She has an entire bookshelf just for her *Lord of the Rings* collections."

"Wow, well, maybe we can get her addicted to hockey." I laugh.

"It'll never happen," she says, looking over at me. A challenging gleam is in her eye.

I narrow my eyes at her. "Challenge accepted."

She laughs and it makes my heart feel light. I love that sound. Melanie washes the last dish and hands it to me. Grabbing the dish from her, our hands brush and our eyes meet. I want to grab her hand and pull her into me like I did at the coffee shop, but she blushes and looks away. I hold back a smile, loving that she's playing hard to get. It's even more appealing to me after dating women like Katarina.

I dry the dish and put it away before walking back over toward Melanie, who's now scrubbing the kitchen sink. I place my hand over hers. "Mel, would you stop?" I chuckle. "My cleaning lady comes tomorrow."

She looks up at me, her face just a few inches from mine. I get a whiff of her shampoo; I want to close my eyes and savor it. It's the same herbal shampoo scent I remember. She clears her throat and takes a step back. Obviously I need to move slowly; I still need to win her trust back.

Trying to lighten the mood, I ask, " Hey, would it be okay if I asked Harrison to stay here? I don't want to cut into your time together, but I have plenty of room." I point toward the stairway leading up to the next level.

"Oh, of course! I'm sure he'd love that. And you're super close to the metro so it wouldn't take him too long to get to my place."

"Did you take the metro here?" My voice comes out louder than I meant it to, causing her eyebrows to raise slightly. Something about Melanie on the metro with all of those strangers this late in the day makes my hackles rise.

She crosses her arms. "I almost always take the metro so I don't have to deal with traffic. I've lived here for several years, West. I know how to look out for myself."

I throw my hands up in defense. "Alright, alright. I'm sorry. I just hate the idea of anything happening to you."

Melanie bites her bottom lip, which just makes me want to kiss her. She runs a hand through her hair and clears her throat. "So, do I get the grand tour?"

"Yeah, sure." I still want to talk to her about the video she sent me. A chill runs through me at the thought. I'm nervous to bring it up since our evening has been so pleasant. But we can't continue brushing this under the rug like it never happened.

She smiles and rushes toward the steps, I laugh at her excitement. She's going to be very disappointed when she realizes how empty the rest of my house is. She stops at the top of the steps and looks back at me. Her lips are twisting like she's about to lecture me. I join her at the top and stick my hands in my pockets. The second floor is empty minus the Xbox, flatscreen TV, and two gaming chairs.

"Really? This is all you have up here?"

I shrug. "My teammates come over sometimes and we game."

She walks over to the TV and picks up an NHL Xbox game case. She looks around for a moment before turning back to me. "This is the *only* game you have?"

I grin. "What did you expect? Besides hockey and an occasional game of golf, I don't have time for hobbies. "

She laughs. "You golf now?"

"I'm not that great, but it's fun to participate in tournaments that raise money for different charities. I even got to golf with Harry Styles last year."

Her jaw drops. "What?? How did I not know about this? I'm *so* jealous."

"I knew you would be." One corner of my mouth pulls up in a smirk. "Come on, let's go up to the third story."

"Okay, but we're not done talking about Harry Styles."

My shoulders shake, trying to suppress a laugh. She looks hesitant to go upstairs, looking down the hallway instead. I say, "There's nothing more on this level, just two empty bedrooms. I'll need to get some furniture before Harrison comes."

She shakes her head. "I can picture you and Harrison staying up late every night playing video games just like you used to."

I smile at the thought; that sounds pretty good to me, except now I have to get up at the crack of dawn to workout and go to practice.

Melanie walks ahead of me up the stairs, and I have to force myself not to check her out. Instead I look down at my feet as I follow her.

She reaches the top of the stars and gasps. "West, this is gorgeous."

I stand next to her and cross my arms in mock offense. "I was really going for rugged and manly."

She laughs. "Okay, rugged and manly and gorgeous."

"Much better." I wink.

She rolls her eyes and walks around my master suite, taking in the details. The entire third story is a cozy master suite with slanted ceilings. It used to be a huge attic, but was converted into the master. The space is way too big for just me, but it's a beautiful and unique. The bay window allows natural light to stream in during the day, but since it's dark outside now, the dark blue curtains are drawn. The walls are painted in the color *linen*—my designer told me that—and the bedding and pillows are white. The decor is more minimalistic in the master than it is downstairs, but there's a large painting hung above my bed. A painting of an azurite stone. It looks like the painting is zoomed in so you can see the brilliant textures and colors of the stone. It's my favorite piece.

Melanie studies the painting for a minute. "You really like these blue stones, huh?"

I look into her big blue eyes, accentuated by her long eyelashes. "Azurite blue is the most beautiful color I've ever seen."

She holds my gaze, a curious expression on her face. She studies me for a second before continuing her tour. She flicks the light on in the master bathroom and gasps again.

"It's completely unfair that you have a bathroom this glamorous. This space is wasted on a man. Have you ever even used that bathtub?!"

I stand next to her in the doorway of the large bathroom. The refurbished claw-foot tub is polished to perfection along with the marble floors. There's a massive steam shower also, that shoots water out in all directions, and everything has the same gold hardware as the rest of my house.

"I have, actually. Soaking in a hot epsom salt bath is great for relaxing sore muscles," I admit. "But I definitely prefer the shower."

She glances from my bare feet to my torso, then back up to my face. Her cheeks turn bright red. The topic of bathing is obviously making her uncomfortable, or embarrassed? I take a few steps back and she follows, turning the bathroom light off as she leaves the room.

Next, she walks over to my dresser where my old laptop rests. She turns to look at me with a bemused expression.

"Despite that big bank account, you still have this ancient laptop?

"It's special." I put my hands in my pockets, feeling nervous.

Her eyes narrow. "How so?"

I swallow slowly and take a deep breath."Because I saved the video you sent me on that laptop."

Her eyes snap open in surprise and her demeanor changes. Gone is the relaxed Melanie, and in her place is anxious Melanie.

"But, why?" she asks, her voice thick with emotion.

Taking a step closer to her, I answer, "Because I was in love with you too. I always have been."

The air between us feels heavy with the unsaid words and feelings of years past. A tear streams down her face and I take two large strides so I'm standing in front of her. I raise my hand to brush the tear from her cheek and, to my surprise, she lets me.

CHAPTER
TWELVE
MELANIE

HOLDING WEST'S INTENSE GAZE, another tear slips free. "Why did you lie to me?"

I hear him sigh heavily. "Besides the stupid pact Harrison and I made?" He pauses and I turn to look at him. "Something Harrison said that day confirmed all my deepest fears, and I convinced I'd be no good for you."

"What did he say?"

"It was right after your appendectomy. Harrison mentioned how upset you were that you couldn't swim. He said with your anxiety, you'd need to be with someone who provided a lot of stability and structure to your life." He drags one hand down his face like he's frustrated with himself. "You always thrived on consistency, and I knew if I played hockey professionally, I couldn't give you that."

My eyebrows draw together, taking in his words.

West starts again. "Once I was drafted, I still had feelings for you, so I put even more distance between us."

I close my eyes and shake my head. My body feels rigid and awkward as I absorb all of this new information. "Wow, teenage boys are really stupid," is all I can manage to say.

He huffs out a nervous laugh, but there's not humor in it. "You're not wrong. But teenage Weston convinced himself you'd be miserable with me *and* I'd lose my best friend."

He sighs and takes my hand in his. His large hand envelopes mine. "I adored your video, Mel. It's embarrassing how many times I've watched it. I'm so sorry for hurting you. I've long since realized I should've given you the chance to decide whether or not my career would be too much for you."

"Yeah, you should've," I tell him, trying to smile as I say it but failing.

"I see you now, living in a completely new city, and thriving. I was wrong to assume what you could or could not." He brings his hand up to cradle my cheek. "I know I hurt you, but I want to earn your trust back. If you'll give me the chance to."

I'm too overwhelmed with emotion to respond. Not just about him wanting to give this a chance, but that he lied to me about his feelings and assumed I was weak. I'm so angry, and yet, I can't think with him this close to me.

Stepping away from him, I turn towards the steps. "I can't even think right now, West. I'm so..." I grind my teeth together to keep my voice from rising. "I'm so angry with you."

He gazes down at his feet, looking ashamed.

A few seconds of silence passes before he adds, "Listen, I know this is a lot to wrap our mind around. I have an early flight in the morning; we have two away games on the west coast." He pauses as if thinking of what to say. "Take some time to think, take all the time you need. And let me know if we can give this a chance? If you can forgive me?"

I stand there, not knowing what to say. We just stare at each other for a moment. Emotions are swirling through my body so fast, I feel dizzy. Once I've finally regained the ability to use my words, I say, "It's late, I need to head home."

"Mel, let me drive you home."

I groan. "I'll be fine, West. I'm *not* weak."

His head rears back like my words were a slap in the face. Ignoring his reaction, I turn and start walking down the stairs.

When I make it to the front door, I slip my heels back on.

"The metro is perfectly safe." I actually hate taking the metro this late, but I refuse to admit that because I'm angry, and hurt, and… and… still infuriatingly attracted to him.

He sighs. "Will you at least drive my car home?"

I roll my lips together. I'd rather drive home than take the metro. "But then what will you drive?"

He wrinkles his nose. "Um… I have more than one car. Do you want to drive the Tesla, the Land Cruiser, or the Mercedes?"

An hour later, I arrive back at my apartment building in West's red Mercedes. I've never been so nervous about parking a vehicle in my life. I put the car in park and breathe a sigh of relief that I drove this beautiful car home safely. It's late and I'm emotionally exhausted, but I know it's going to take me hours to fall asleep.

No amount of essential oils or weighted blankets can take away my anxious thoughts or the hurt twisting my stomach.

———

When my alarm goes off early the next morning, I feel like I've been hit by a truck. Overthinking and tossing and turning in your bed can make you so exhausted.

Forcing myself out of bed, I grab my peppermint essential oil. I inhale the refreshing scent, then dap a few drops on my temples to soothe my throbbing headache.

I'm relieved West will be out of town for a few days so I can process everything he said last night. I need to decide if I can forgive him and move forward. If I can learn to trust him again.

And if I'm being honest with myself, I really don't *know* if I can handle the whirlwind of being with a professional athlete. So were his doubts completely unfounded?

The more I think about it, I wonder if Harrison had a point. I *do* thrive on schedules and organization. But then again, just because something is difficult, doesn't mean it's impossible.

Looking in the mirror, I almost gasp at my reflection. My hair is all over the place like a bird's nest, and the dark circles under my eyes make me look about eighty years old. I dress myself in some plaid trousers and a white sweater before walking out to the kitchen. Noel is already awake and has the kettle warming up on the stovetop.

Ahh, she knows me too well. She's way more of a morning person than I am; you can't even tell she just woke up. She already has her blonde curls tamed and she's dressed for work in black dress pants, a classic white button-up, and brown suspenders. Noel is an old soul, and her outfits definitely reflect that.

"Good morning!" she chirps. "How was dinner last night?"

I blow out a breath. "I have so much to tell you, I don't even know where to start."

"Start at the beginning!" she tells me before filling two teacups with hot water from the kettle.

I recount the details of my evening with West, from dinner and the house tour to his admission that he lied about not having feelings for me. "He said he was in love with me then... and that he *still* is."

Her jaw drops. "Wow." Her eyes gloss over with tears. "Why'd you have to make me cry before six AM?"

I grimace. "Sorry, but you asked." Taking a tea bag from the box on the counter, I steep it in my hot water. "I just don't know how to sort through my feelings about all of this."

She scoffs. "Why are you not running over to his house and telling him you want to have all of his babies?"

"I forgot how much of a romantic you are," I say with a laugh then take a sip of tea. "Like the whole thing with Katarina? I'd have to deal with every female who wants to sink her claws into him. And public attention, and tabloids, and him traveling all the time." I widen my eyes for dramatic effect.

Noel nods in understanding. "Yeah, being with someone that famous would definitely have its challenges. I guess you need to decide if you'd rather be with West and face the hardships... or be without him."

"Being without him does sound pretty awful." I take a deep breath. "He's out of town for a few days. He told me to think about this while he's gone."

She swallows a sip of her own tea. "You have a lot to process."

"I need to get ready for work. Thanks for being my sounding board." I smile and she steps toward me and pulls me into a big hug.

Still hugging me, Noel whispers, "Can I please order shirts that say #KissinKershaw?"

CHAPTER
THIRTEEN
WEST

USUALLY, I love traveling for away games. Seeing a new city and playing in a different arena is exciting. But this time, I'm just anxious about what Melanie is thinking. She looked so devastated when I admitted to lying about my feelings years ago. And I feel like an idiot for thinking she couldn't handle my career when she's obviously an intelligent and independent woman.

Instead of letting her make her own choice, I made the choice for her. And I feel like a huge jerk for doing that. She's right... teenaged boys *are* stupid.

This lifestyle isn't easy for any of us. Between our intense training schedule and traveling, my teammates with wives and kids have it the hardest. Having to be away from their families all the time has to be challenging. But I guess at the end of the day, it's worth it when you get to go back home to the ones you love.

And that's what I'd for for me and Mel. To come home to her after long trips, to hold her in my arms...

Today, my team and I are flying from northern California to southern California. We won our game last night and are hoping for another win tonight. I'm seated next to Remy. He's a big guy, probably an inch or two taller than me, so I'm grateful the Eagles charter a jet with large, comfortable seats. Remy is one of those guys who walks into a room and commands attention, without saying a word. With his dark hair, and penetrating brown eyes, everything about him screams *leader*. Bruce, our goalie, and Colby are across from us. Mitch is snoring behind us, avoiding everyone, as usual.

We've started up a game of Exploding Kittens—yeah, we're not as cool as we seem—and while I'm waiting for them to shuffle and deal a new game, I write in the journal I started for Melanie. I've been writing letters to her every day and will give her the leather-bound journal when I get back home tomorrow night.

"Put your diary away, West. It's your turn," Colby teases with a laugh.

Bruce blows his blonde hair out of his eyes, he needs a haircut. Not sure how he blocked so many goals during last night's game with that blonde mop in his eyes. "What's with the diary, anyway?"

I draw a card and then slide the notebook back into my backpack. "It's a *journal*," I correct. "And I'm just amending some mistakes I made years ago."

Bruce quirks a brow. "Ah, the plot thickens."

"This have anything to do with that Congressman's assistant?" Colby asks.

I shrug.

Remy curses under his breath. "Would you two leave him alone?" He plays an attack card and Bruce draws two cards, glaring at Remy the entire time. But Bruce's smirk and twinkle in his blue eyes gives away that he's not actually that upset.

My phone pings with a text and I grab it out of my pocket so quickly the guys stare at me with their eyebrows raised in question. When I see it's just a text from Harrison, I try my hardest to push away my disappointment. I should've known it'd be a text from him and not Mel since I texted him this morning telling him he can stay at my place when he's in town.

HARRISON

That'd be great, man. Just like college, except a nicer crib. *gif of Snoop Dog throwing money around*

HARRISON

BTW what's new with you and Mel?

WEST

Still working on it.

HARRISON

She's a tough one.

WEST

Yep, always has been.

Smiling to myself, I put my phone away. Harrison is right; Melanie is a tough one. She's not one to swoon over pretty words without really thinking about the words and who said them. I like that she's a thinker and a planner. When Melanie makes a decision, you know she's 100% certain about it. I'm just crossing my fingers she can be 100% certain about *us*.

My phone starts playing One Direction's "One Thing," which is my ringtone for Melanie.

Colby rolls his blue eyes and tosses his cards onto the small table. "We're never going to finish the game at this rate," he mutters.

I silently mouth a sorry to the boys before answering. "Hello? Mel?"

"Hey, West. Did I catch you at a bad time?"

"I'll always have time for you," I say with fervor.

Remy scoffs next to me and Colby mutters "whipped" but disguises it with a cough.

She laughs but it sounds strained like she's nervous. "Alright. How was your game?"

"You don't watch my games?" The guys burst out laughing at my question, and I wish I wouldn't have asked it.

"Uh, not usually." I can hear the regret in her voice. "Sorry…"

"That's okay, no big deal." I try to sound cool and unaffected, but on the inside, I want to cry a little.

She clears her throat. "So, I was wondering if we could talk tomorrow? After I get off work?"

My heart rate speeds up. She wants to talk… isn't it always bad when someone says they want to talk? But we do need to talk, so hopefully, it's a good kind of talk. "Yeah, of course. I'm free tomorrow evening."

"My roommate is teaching an evening class tomorrow, so do you want to come over here?"

"Sounds good. I'm excited to see your place." I smile, forgetting my teammates are listening.

The three of them chuckle. Bruce leans forward, causing his long brown hair to fall into his eyes, and he whispers, "Oooh going to *her* place. It's getting serious." I shoot him a glare.

"Don't get too excited. It's nothing like your place." Melanie laughs, her voice starting to sound more relaxed.

"I'm guessing that means you actually have furniture in all the rooms?" I ask.

"It's definitely filled to maximum capacity," she says

sarcastically. "Hey, could you take the metro here, or an Uber? Then you can drive your car back home."

"Are you sure? You're welcome to use it. I don't mind."

"Thanks, but I have a car. I just prefer the metro to avoid traffic... and parallel parking."

I smirk, remembering her parallel parking in front of the cafe. "Understandable. Text me your address and I'll be there tomorrow."

"Okay, see you tomorrow."

We end the call and I feel lighter. The weight of wondering if she'd want to see me again no longer looming over me. She sounded positive, so hopefully, that's a good sign.

Tomorrow night I'll find out if she'll give me a chance... or if I need to keep fighting.

CHAPTER
FOURTEEN
MELANIE

AFTER ARRIVING HOME FROM SWIMMING, I make a protein smoothie for dinner and then walk back to my bedroom so I can FaceTime my mom. I was feeling jittery today, so I swam laps before coming home. Swimming has been just as therapeutic as I remembered. I felt much calmer afterward. But water can't give me advice, and my mom can. Plus, she already knows about the infamous video and the history between West and me.

She seemed so sure back then that West reciprocated my feelings. I'm interested to hear her thoughts on him now, even though five years have passed.

While I wait for the video to connect, I settle back on my bed and get comfortable. When Mom's face pops up on the screen, she's holding her phone down on her lap and adjusting her glasses. Even though she's holding her phone at an unflattering angle, she still looks lovely to me.

"Hello, sweetheart!" She smiles broadly.

"Hey, Mom!" I smile back. "I miss you."

Dad pops into the frame and waves. "How's my baby girl?"

I laugh. "Hey, Dad. I miss you too."

"When are you moving back to Minnesota? You're too far away, don't you know?" Dad asks with a wink.

I roll my eyes. "I know. I know. If only there were some job openings for political assistants there."

Dad chuckles. "Okay, I'll let you two beautiful ladies chat. Love you, Mel."

"Love you too, Dad!" I wave and he grins.

Once it's just me and Mom, she studies me through the screen. "What's on your mind? I can tell there's something you want to talk about."

I nod. "I can never hide anything from you, can I?"

"Nope, it's a mother's superpower, reading her children." She smirks and slides her glasses down to the tip of her nose. "This doesn't happen to be about a certain Weston Kershaw, does it?"

My eyes narrow at her but she just keeps smiling. "How did you know?"

"His mother told me you two had coffee."

Of course our moms have already talked about this. I resist rolling my eyes. "Yeah, we did. Well, tea for me. But he also had me over for dinner."

"And?" She leans toward the screen like she's on the edge of her seat.

I bite my bottom lip. "He basically told me he's always loved me." I hug the pillow tight and wait for her response.

"Well, it's about time he admitted it." She blows out a deep breath. "You know, boys' brains don't finish developing until they're twenty-five. So it would make sense he finally figured things out now."

I'm going to have to Google that later and see if it's true. I bet it is.

"But Mom…" I pause.

"What's the matter?" Her eyebrows furrow in concern.

"I'm worried my anxiety mixed with West's lifestyle is a recipe for disaster. I mean, I almost had a panic attack when people were taking photos of us at that cafe." I sigh. "Oh, and the women that fawn all over him. What if I can't handle it?"

"Melanie, you've always been able to do anything you put your mind to. Sure, you can be structured, but you're also determined. If it's West you want, you'll find a way." She smiles at me the way she always has, the smile that seems to make everything okay.

"I do want West."

Her smile grows, making her cheeks push her glasses up slightly. "You can bring some stability into his chaos. I think you could help each other grow."

I laugh. "I hope you're right."

Mom nods and we continue chatting for a few minutes before she has to leave for her book club. We end the call and I'm feeling more confident about what I want to say to West tomorrow.

———

The next day, I'm a total wreck at work. I spilled coffee on my shirt, sent an email to Madden that was supposed to go to the senator of Indiana, and put an appointment into Madden's schedule at the wrong time—causing him to miss said appointment.

He seems more concerned about my well-being than he is upset by my mistakes. I've had to assure him numerous times that I'm alright and I don't need to take a sick day.

When it's finally six p.m., I gather my things and say goodbye to Madden. I walk a few blocks to my favorite restaurant to pick up my to-go order of chicken quinoa bowls for dinner. This place uses all organic and free range ingredients, so nothing that should trigger my anxiety. West made dinner last time, so I'm taking care of dinner tonight. I'd cook something, but it's already past six and I'm not even home yet.

Thirty minutes later, I'm walking into my apartment. It's quiet since Noel teaches an evening class once a week. I made sure to clean and tidy the place up last night so it would look decent when West arrived. Not that it was ever messy to begin with. I mostly just had to pick up Noel's things and toss them in her room. Okay, I didn't toss them in there; I put everything away neatly. I couldn't help it.

Looking at the clock in the kitchen, I calculate how much time I have to change out of my coffee-stained shirt from work. Eight minutes. Perfect. I rush back to my room, take off my work clothes, and pull on some black leggings, a grey v-neck tee, and a plaid button-down. I glance in the mirror and give my hair a little fluff and freshen up my lipstick. A knock comes from the front door and my stomach flips.

Inhaling a deep breath, I walk down the hallway toward the front door. I peek through the peephole and see West filling the hallway with his large frame. He shuffles from his left foot to his right foot like he's nervous. Glad I'm not the only one.

I open the door. Once he sees me, his shoulders visibly relax and he smiles. "Hey, Mel." He pulls me into a hug, enveloping me in his warmth, and my nerves are forgotten.

He pulls away just enough to kiss me on the cheek, and the feel of his soft lips makes me feel warm and tingly all over. Which is more of a response than I ever had with my ex, Jeff.

"I'm glad you're back. Come on in."

He steps inside and I close the door behind us. West closes

his eyes and inhales. "It smells like you in here. I don't know if I've ever told you this, but I love the scent of your shampoo."

I smile and try not to blush. Unsuccessfully. "Thank you. It's organic and infused with essential oils."

"I'll have to get some." He smirks. "This is a great apartment, and the neighborhood looks safe."

"Don't worry, your Mercedes still has all of its tires."

He takes a step toward me. "I only care about *your* safety. The car doesn't matter."

"Did you mean everything you said the other night?" I blurt out before I can stop myself.

"I meant every word. I love you, Mel," he says, his expression serious. "I have something for you." He reaches back and takes a small leather notebook out of his back pocket.

"I've been writing you letters every day in this journal." He hands it to me.

It's a lovely leather journal with an intricate floral design, and my name is engraved on the corner. "Wow, thank you. It's beautiful."

"Every time I have to leave for away games, I'll take it with me and write to you. When I get back, I'll give it to you to read."

My vision becomes blurry with unshed tears. I blink rapidly, trying to urge the tears away.

West places a hand under my chin and nudges my face up to look at him. "I have five years to make up for."

I throw my arms around his neck and hug him tightly. West's arms wrap around my waist and we stand there embracing each other in my tiny living room for several minutes. Wow, it feels good to be held by him. Better than eighteen-year-old Melanie ever could've imagined.

"I'm so sorry for hurting you," he whispers into my neck.

I pull back slightly so I can see his face. "I forgive you." I pause, biting my bottom lip. "And I'd like to give this a try, West. Give us a try. It won't be easy, but I think it could be worth it."

He closes his eyes and presses his forehead against mine. "I'm so relieved to hear you say that."

I look into his eyes and am overcome with emotion. I've dreamt of this moment for so long, and never thought it would happen, never thought we'd actually be together. But here we are. I stand on my toes and place a kiss on his lips. Before I can pull away, West tightens his grip on my waist and pulls me into him. His lips are soft and warm, and he smells like pine needles and leather. His short beard prickles the soft skin on my cheeks. All of my senses are alive and humming.

I sigh in contentment then feel West tilt his head for a better angle and I thread my fingers through the hair at his nape. It's thick and soft, just like I always dreamed it would be.

Too soon, West pulls away slowly but keeps his arms around my waist. "Wow," he says with a grin.

"Wow." I echo.

"So, are we dating now?" he asks.

I giggle. "Um yeah, I hope so. I don't often kiss men that I'm not dating."

"Okay, whew."

A thought pops into my head and my eyes widen. "Oh my gosh, what are we going to tell Harrison?"

West bites his lip. "Well, he kind of already knows."

"What? How?" I ask, my fists going to my hips.

"It's Bro Code. I had to get his permission." He sticks his hands into his pockets. "And also he saw the photos from the cafe…"

I groan. "Ugh, I'd almost forgotten about those."

He waggles his eyebrows "So, what do we do now?"

"I got quinoa bowls for us to eat," I tell him.

He quirks a brow. "No, I mean with us. Our relationship."

"Oh, right. So, dating a professional athlete is new to me. I'm going to need you to be patient."

He nods. "I get that. Like the whole Katarina thing."

I take a deep breath. "Yeah, and women making marriage proposal signs. And your crazy schedule. And the attention…"

He rubs the back of his neck with one hand. "Yeah, it's a lot. It took time for me to get used to it too, so I understand."

My stomach rumbles loudly, making us laugh. "So, about dinner…" I gesture to the table where the bag from the restaurant sits.

West and I sit and eat together, enjoying the simplicity of just being in each other's company. When we're finished, we move to the sofa and turn on a movie. He puts an arm around me and I lay my head on his sturdy shoulder. West plays with my hair, which is incredibly soothing. I have no idea what movie is even playing on the small TV. All I know is West is here with me and he loves me.

The sound of the front door opening draws our attention. Noel emerges from the hallway. Her mouth turns up into a wide grin. "Well, if it isn't Weston Kershaw."

West smiles at her and says, "Lovelui na govannon- cin."

Noel's jaw drops and she looks from me to West and then back at me again. "He knows elvish?!" She whisper-yells. "This man is marriage material, Mel."

West sits beside me with a devilish grin on his handsome face. "How do you know elvish?" I ask, crossing my arms.

"I knew I'd have to win your roommate over somehow," he whispers. "Now, if we can just get her to like hockey."

"I heard that!" Noel says defensively. "Not going to happen."

We laugh at her dramatics.

She waves a hand at us dismissively. "Alright, it was nice meeting you, West. I'll leave you two love birds alone."

"Nice meeting you too, Noel." He tells her before turning back toward me.

Noel's bedroom door clicks shut and West's hand comes up to caress my face, his thumb and forefinger gliding along my jawline and then along my bottom lip.

"I believe we have years of kissing to catch up on," he whispers, his voice low and husky.

"Is that right?"

One corner of his lips pull up in a grin and then he kisses me, soft and slow. I bring my hands to his face, angling his head where I want him. I stop the kiss and lean back, just far enough to where I can look into his eyes. "West?"

"Yes, Melanie?" His voice comes out in a raspy whisper.

"I love you too."

His eyes soften and he kisses me again and again and again.

———

By the time West leaves and I head to bed, it's nearly 1 a.m. He's going to be exhausted for practice tomorrow, and I'm going to feel like a zombie at work.

But it was worth it. It was the evening of my dreams, literally. Except it was even better because when I wake up, I'll know it wasn't just a dream.

Despite the fact that it's late, I'm dying to read the notes he wrote me in the journal. I settle into bed after washing my face and throwing on an oversized, comfy T-shirt, and open the journal.

· · ·

Mel,

I thought I'd start this journal off by telling you three of my favorite things about you.

1. You love following schedules, which makes you very reliable. This quality is surprisingly hot.

2. You always make sure everything is tidy and organized. No picture frames will ever be crooked on your watch.

3. You smell like essential oils. So every time I'm near you, it's like I'm at a spa.

P.S. I love Wesanie for a couple name.
    -West

I giggle at the last part then close the journal and hug it to my chest. I sigh, feeling so happy and content. I never knew how much I needed someone to love the quirks about me.

The very things I dislike about myself the most. But West knows my struggles and loves me anyway.

CHAPTER
FIFTEEN
WEST

TWO DAYS LATER, I'm pacing around my living room, waiting for Harrison and Melanie to arrive. Harrison's flight got in an hour ago and Mel is picking him up then heading over here for a pizza and movie night. I just saw her last night, and I still spent the entire day missing her.

The thought of the three of us hanging out together again has put a grin on my face all day. Hopefully I can sneak in some more kisses without Harrison noticing. Not sure I can resist Melanie's sweet lips now that I've had a taste of them. I guess Harrison will just have to deal with it.

Finally, the doorbell rings and I practically run to answer it. Harrison comes right inside, wheeling his suitcase behind him.

He pulls me into a hug and we slap each other on the back. "Good to see you, man," he tells me.

I pull away and smile. "You too. It's been too long."

Melanie closes the door behind her, looking shy. This thing between us has been years in the making, but it also feels so new. I'm sure this is strange for her, especially with her brother around.

I, on the other hand, am not shy or embarrassed at all. I

loop my hands around her waist and she gasps when I pick her up so her feet are off the ground. "I missed you today." I nuzzle my nose in the crook of her neck, inhaling the sweet scent of her soft skin.

She giggles and I plant a kiss right on her pretty, pink lips. Her sweetness is addicting. She's blushing so hard, and I'll probably keep embarrassing her just to keep that blush there.

Harrison clears his throat and we turn our heads to look at him. "It's definitely going to take me a minute to get used to this." He runs a hand through his dark hair then looks down at his feet.

I set Melanie back on the ground, but grab her hand. Turning my attention back to Harrison, I say, "Come upstairs and check out your guest suite."

Grinning, I lead them toward the stairs. Harrison is eyeing our joined hands with an odd expression. We walk up the stairs and down the short hallway to one of the bedrooms and I open the door. I had furniture delivered and set up while I was traveling.

Harrison steps inside the room and bursts out laughing, his deep chuckle filling the room. "Really?" he asks, still laughing.

The queen size bed is donned with red D.C. Eagles bedding and pillows. Above the bed hangs two criss-crossed hockey sticks, and above the nightstands are my framed jerseys: one from the Washington Eagles, and another from the Quebec Wolverines. I also hung several posters of myself around the room just to annoy him.

Melanie laughs. "Wow. West, your inner designer really came out in here."

With a smirk, I nod in agreement. "Yeah, I'm thinking of retiring early from hockey and going into interior design."

Harrison rolls his eyes, but one side of his mouth is quirked in a smile.

"Could you do my place next? I could use some of these posters." Melanie looks up at me and bats her eyelashes. "Especially if you have one from your shirtless zamboni photo shoot."

I wink at her. "You can have all the posters you want. I even have a life-sized cardboard cutout of myself that would brighten up your living room."

"Perfect." She giggles.

Harrison ignores us and tosses his suitcase on the bed. "Okay, where's the pizza? I'm starving."

We head back down to the kitchen and dig into the pizza I had delivered just before they arrived. I even managed to find bottles of the same old-fashioned root beer we used to drink as kids.

Harrison swallows a bite and takes a swig of his root beer. "You know, this feels surprisingly normal. Even though you two can't stop staring at each other."

"You're right. It's been too long since the three of us hung out." I smile at Melanie. "And now I don't have to hide my feelings for your sister."

Melanie blushes again while we grin at each other.

Harrison quirks an eyebrow. "You could hide it a *little* bit, you know."

I shake my head. "Not a chance."

After finishing our dinner, we head back upstairs where the T.V. is. I grab the remote and pull Netflix up. "Alright, what movie are we feeling tonight?"

"How about *The Three Musketeers*?" Harrison says with a smile.

Melanie nods. "Seems fitting."

"*The Three Musketeers* it is!" I push play before sitting down in one of the gaming chairs.

"There are only two chairs, so Mel you take this one. I'll sit on the floor." Harrison nudges the chair towards her.

Before she can sit, I grab her wrist and pull her onto my lap. "Nonsense, no need for anyone to sit on the floor."

"West!" Melanie resists, but her grin tells me she doesn't mind so much.

She relaxes and rests her head on my shoulder. I lay my head on top of hers and take a deep breath to smell her hair.

Harrison wrinkles his nose. "You two really aren't easing me into this slowly, are you?" He takes a seat. "I guess I need to get a girlfriend so I'm not a third wheel."

I shake my head at how dramatic he is then we all quiet down as the movie starts.

Once Harrison is immersed in the movie, I brush my lips against a sweet little spot right behind Melanie's ear. "So, you liked the Zamboni photos, huh?" I whisper.

I feel her head move up and down in a nod. "That photo shoot lives rent-free in my head."

Smiling against her neck, I reply, "You know, I could give you a live remake of that photo shoot."

She giggles. "Only if I'm the one who gets to oil you up."

"It's a deal. Bring your essential oils. Lavender is my favorite."

A loud exaggerated sigh comes from Harrison. "You guys realize I can hear you, right?"

Pulling my head back so I can look at Mel, she meets my gaze and we both grimace. "Sorry, Harrison," we say in unison.

Melanie snuggles back into my chest and I place a kiss on the top of her head. She releases a contented sigh, and I wrap my arms around her waist like I'm never letting go.

CHAPTER
SIXTEEN
MELANIE

THE WEEK after Harrison's visit was busy, West had to travel to Canada for three away games, and I've been busy running the office while Madden is out of town.

It's Saturday morning and I tried my hardest to sleep in and recuperate from a hectic week. But when West got in late last night, he called to tell me he has a special date planned for us today.

How's a girl supposed to sleep in when her man plans an exciting surprise date? She can't. It's not possible.

He told me to dress warm, so I'm wearing my fleece-lined black leggings and the D.C. Eagles hoodie I stole from West. I'm slipping on some fuzzy socks when I hear the doorbell. I slip and slide on the wood floor as I run down the hallway to open the door.

West stands on the other side of the door with a nervous smile on his face. He shifts from one foot to the other and sticks his hands in the pockets of his black jogger pants.

"What's wrong?" I ask him, feeling apprehensive at his nervous body language.

He bites his bottom lip and steps inside the apartment.

"Well, last week you mentioned to me and Harrison that you'd like to try ice skating again… indoors, of course."

I gulp. "Okay…"

"So, I planned an ice skating date. But on the drive over here I started freaking out that it might be too much, and I don't want to pressure you into getting back on the ice." He takes my hand in his and softly rubs the back of my hand with his thumb. "So, the decision is yours. We can go ice skating, or do something else."

I pull my hand away so I can wrap my arms around him. He relaxes instantly and embraces me in a warm hug.

"First of all, I freaking missed you," I say, and then feel his chuckle rumble through his chest.

"I missed you too." He gives me a squeeze and kisses the top of my head.

"Secondly, I appreciate you giving me the choice. And I would like to try ice skating again."

He pulls back to look me in the eye. "Are you sure?"

"I'm sure. Even if I just step out there and don't have a panic attack, it'll be a win." I smile. "And who better to go with than a professional hockey player?"

He grins. "True. And I just *happen* to be a professional hockey player."

Half an hour later, West parks at the skating rink. I notice the parking lot is empty except for one other vehicle. "Um, are you sure it's open?"

He shoots me a tight smile. "Yeah… I actually rented the whole place for the day."

"Are you serious?" I quirk a brow at him.

"Yep. And I got you a present!" He winks then gets out of the car and grabs a large box from the trunk.

I get out and see he's holding a box containing brand new

hockey skates. "West, you didn't have to get me skates. I could've just used the rentals!"

"Mel, I mean this in the least snobby way possible," he pauses to take a deep breath. "No girlfriend of mine will ever be seen in rental skates."

I bite the insides of my cheeks to keep from laughing, but only because I can tell he's totally serious. The idea of rental skates is *that* horrible to him.

"Well, thank you. These are lovely." I trace my finger along the sparkly pink laces.

West smiles, looking pleased with himself. "Great, they're freshly sharpened too. You take these and I'll grab my skates."

He hands me my new skates, grabs a duffle bag from the trunk and we head inside. The lady at the front desk, who's probably in her seventies, shoots West a knowing smile and he winks at her.

"You're a shameless flirt, Weston Kershaw." I make a tsking sound with my tongue.

"You jealous of me and Mabel?" He says while waggling his eyebrows.

I giggle and we find a bench to lace our skates up. West gets down on a knee to tie mine, his hands and fingers brushing against my calves. The cold air in the skating rink is no match for the warmth that surges through my veins when West touches me. He looks up and meets my gaze, one edge of his lips curving into a mischievous smile.

"Keep looking at me like that, and all of the ice in this place is going to melt before I even get to use my new skates."

West chuckles then comes and sits next to me so he can lace up his own skates. "Alright, I'll behave."

Now that I'm not distracted by West's touch, I start feeling nervous. I know I cannot fall through this ice, but the anxiety will override the logical part of my brain if I let it. I take a few deep breaths before I feel West's palm on the back of my neck. He massages it gently.

"You okay? Say the word and we'll leave."

"No, I'm okay. I need to do this."

We stand and make our way over to the rink. The air gets colder the closer we get, by the time we're right in front of the ice, we can see our own breath. My body starts shaking, not because I'm cold, but because I'm terrified.

West steps onto the ice and reaches for my hands. "Just remember, the ice isn't even an inch thick, and underneath is just cement."

"You're right. I can do this."

I squeeze my eyes closed, and step onto the ice slowly, one foot at a time. I'm gripping West's hands so tight I'm probably cutting off his circulation. I take a slow steadying breath then open my eyes.

West is smiling at me. "Look at you, facing your fears. I'm so proud of you."

My eyes blur with tears and a breathy laugh escapes my lungs. West begins to skate backward, pulling me along with him.

My heart is beating so fast. I'm half scared and half excited. But I feel so safe with West by my side.

He continues to pull me around the ice until I feel more at ease. I let go of his hands and stand there for a moment, looking at the wide expanse of the rink. I breathe in the cold air and start to glide on my own.

West skates up next to me with a big smile and the lights begin to dim. One Direction's first album starts playing over the sound system and I burst into laughter.

"You're never going to let me forget my One Direction phase, are you?"

"Never." He laughs.

We continue skating hand in hand, belting out the lyrics to the songs. The longer we skate, the calmer I feel.

"Thank you for this. I don't think I could've done it without you."

"You could have, because you're strong and amazing." He squeezes my hand. "But thank you for trusting me."

He stops and spins to face me, pulling me toward him easily. He bends down and smiles against my lips before kissing me. His warmth enveloping me completely.

I don't think I'll ever be cold again with this man by my side.

EPILOGUE, 7 MONTHS LATER

WEST

MY HEART BOOMS in my chest as I drive down the long, winding driveway toward the cabin I purchased last week. Nervous excitement is making me jittery... or maybe that's the five cups of coffee I drank this morning.

I've never looked so forward to the off-season, but the past seven months, I've been counting down the days.

Do I still love hockey? Yes.

Am I excited to start training camp in a few months? Of course.

But am I going to soak up my summer off and all the time I get to spend with Melanie? ABSOLUTELY.

Usually, Mel would be hard at work campaigning with Madden Windell and his team, but he decided not to run for reelection. Knowing how difficult it has been for him to be away from his family so much, she understood. But was still disappointed.

I'm sad for Mel, I really am. I know she loved that job. But this gave us both the opportunity to have the summer off together. Which means, perfect timing for me to put a ring on her finger. A wide grin spreads across my face at the thought.

Driving past a row of long pine trees, the large, two-story cabin comes into view. Cabin is an understatement for this grandiose property. Mel will probably tease me relentlessly about how ostentatious it is. But we need room for all the kids we're going to have. My heart pounds again when I picture a cute little girl with pigtails and big blue eyes, just like Melanie.

Okay, you're getting a little ahead of yourself, man. Propose first.

I park my vehicle and pull the black velvet box out of my shorts pocket. Opening the box, I stare at the ring I've been carrying around all day. A ring so perfect for Mel, I couldn't resist purchasing it only a month after we started officially dating. I saw it in a store window and stopped in my tracks. The large emerald-cut diamond is gorgeous, but it's the side stones that drew my attention. Three small sapphires on each side, almost the same color as Melanie's eyes.

Mel is meeting me here in an hour, so I need to get everything set up quickly. She must be getting used to my spontaneity, because she didn't even question me when I asked her to meet me at a random address.

I walk around the house, once again amazed by the beauty of the property. Right on the lake, surrounded by trees. The cabin itself is impressive, but it's the grounds that sold it for me. I could instantly picture me and Melanie here. In my head, we'll spend every summer at the cabin, away from the city and only twenty minutes from our families. I can visualize our future children running around by the lake, our parents coming over for bonfires… annnnnd maybe an indoor ice rink made with synthetic ice. For the kiddos, not for me. Okay a little for me.

———

Melanie

I'm sitting in my car in front of a rustic mansion... one might perhaps call it a cabin? But it's a very, very fancy cabin. I check the address West texted me once more.

"What on earth?" I whisper to myself.

I can see a small white sign taped to the front door so I get out of my car to investigate. The property is obviously several acres, because I can't see any other homes from where I stand, and the only sounds I hear are the chirping of birds followed by a light breeze.

When I reach the front door, I read the note.

Mel, come on in.
-W

"Hmm." I purse my lips and twist the door handle. The door is heavy and nearly twice my height, but it opens easily and I walk inside the foyer.

I look down and see a trail of paper arrows. I'm assuming West placed them here, so I follow them with an amused smile on my face. West is always full of surprises. Who knows what he's up to. Being with him has shown me that I don't always have to be in control. Sometimes life is more fun when it's unplanned.

I continue following the arrows down a long hallway until I reach a huge, open room. There's an impressive kitchen and large island, but the rest of the space is empty, like the whole house seems to be.

Turning in a circle to glance around the room, I spot a projector screen above the fireplace. The video is paused, so it's just West's smiling face filling the screen.

Taking a few steps toward the projector, I notice there's another note, and next to it lies a single red rose and a remote. I pick the note up to read it with a big grin. This is so fun... like a scavenger hunt.

Press play.
-W

Grabbing the remote with a big smile, I press play and the video of West starts.

"Hey, Mel. I thought it was fitting to do this via video." He winks at the camera. "I realize we've only been dating for about seven months. But I don't think I can wait another moment to make you my wife."

I feel my eyebrows shoot up to my hairline and realize my mouth is open as I gape at the video.

West continues talking on the recording, "I love you more than anything in the world, Melanie." Video-West is looking deep into my eyes like he's here in person. How is it that just a recording can make my heart leap?

"You're the only one for me. Marry me, please?" The recording stops, and I'm left standing there breathless.

Happy tears brim in my eyes and I hear the clearing of a throat coming from behind me. I whip around and West is standing there looking impossibly handsome in worn jeans and a D.C. Eagles jersey. His teary eyes are mirroring my own and we're both grinning at each other like fools.

"Yes!" I yell as I rush toward him. "I'll marry you."

He catches me in his arms and spins me around the large, open room. He comes to a stop, sets me down and pulls a little box out of his jeans pocket. When he opens it I gasp. The ring is more perfect than I ever could have imagined.

"Are those sapphires?" I ask as he slips the ring on my finger.

He nods. "I wanted azurite since they match your eyes *exactly*... but I saw this with the sapphires and knew it was the ring for you."

Realization dawns on me when he mentions azurite. "Are the stones on your mantle azurite?"

He chuckles softly. "Yeah. They're the exact same color as your eyes."

"And the painting above your bed?"

He wrinkles his nose and scratches the top of his head. "Am I creepy?"

I burst out laughing and stand on my toes so I can wrap my arms around him. "No! That is the sweetest thing I've ever heard."

"Okay, glad you think it's sweet and not serial killer-ish." He leans down and whispers, "Now shut up and kiss me, Mel." His warm breath and lips against my ear sends a shiver down my spine.

I tilt my head to look at him, taking in those familiar grey-blue eyes and scruff-covered jaw. I can't believe this man is going to be mine for life. Leaning forward, I gently brush my lips against his, savoring this moment.

His hands go to my waist and pull me tight against him. Our height difference causes me to crane my neck and stand on my tippy-toes, making it impossible for me to get as close as I'd like.

West must be a mind-reader because he hoists me up so I can wrap my legs around his waist. He bites my bottom lip, making me gasp. I can feel his smile against my mouth and I can't help but smile as well.

Before I even realize he was walking, he has moved us into the kitchen and sets me down on the counter, but keeps his arms around my waist and continues exploring my lips with his. West slows our kisses and pulls back a few inches. I groan at the loss of his warmth, making him chuckle.

"Gotta save some of that for the wedding night, Mel." He waggles his index finger and shakes his head like he's reprimanding me, and I roll my eyes.

I groan. "Can we just elope right now?"

West leans his forehead against mine and sighs. "I'd love that. But I have a feeling our families would be a little unhappy if we excluded them."

"Yeah, you're right." I agree. "But I'm so tired of saying goodbye to you each night. I want to kiss you goodnight and fall asleep right by your side."

He pulls back and his eyes are dark. "Oh, I definitely want you right beside me, but I have a few things in mind that would be *way* more fun than sleep."

My body heats and I'm positive I'm blushing like never before.

Hesitantly, West takes a step back, putting a little distance between us. My eyes probably look so feral he thinks I'm going to jump him right here in this empty house.

Speaking of house... He holds his arms out and does a slow spin around he empty room. "So, what do you think of our new house?"

"Wait, this is ours?" My eyebrows raise as I glance around the large space. I'm seeing the cabin with a fresh outlook now, filled with furniture, West and I cozied up by the fireplace after putting our children to bed.

"I love it."

West beams at me for a moment, eyeing me quizzically from top to bottom.

"What?" I demand. "You're being weird."

He rubs his chin the places his fists on his hips. "Something's missing."

I hold up my left hand to flash my sparkly ring. "Isn't this all I need?"

He tilts his head back and laughs before walking toward the nearest kitchen cabinet and opening it. "I know what you need."

West pulls a red jersey from the cabinet and comes back with a mischievous grin that makes him look boyish and adorable. That's when I notice the number on his jersey, and the one he's carrying isn't his signature number 22. Instead, the shoulders are embellished with heart patches. He hands me the jersey he's carrying and I see it matches his own.

"Look at the back." He crosses his arms and waits expectantly.

I flip the shirt and start laughing so hard I can barely breathe. He laughs with me and spins so I can see the back of his red jersey says "Wesanie" just like mine does.

Once I can finally speak again, I say, "I don't know whether to be amused or humiliated."

He grimaces. "Hopefully amused… because everyone will be here in a few minutes and they're wearing these jerseys."

My eyes widen. "Who's *everyone*??"

———

An hour later, we're surrounded by friends and family, all donning their *Wesanie* jerseys.

Our parents are here, along with West's two older sisters, Bristol and Hannah. Noel and Harrison even flew in for the occasion, along with two of West's teammates, Ford Remington, the team captain, and Colby Knight, West's closest friend on the team. The poor guy has been flirting incessantly with Noel. Unsuccessfully, I might add.

"So, where did the term *Wesanie* come from anyway?" Harrison asks before taking a sip of the celebratory champagne we opened.

West's sisters and teammates lean in, obviously curious as well.

I give them a brief synopsis of my drug-induced declaration of love. Ford and Colby laugh and slap West on the back like he's the man. And his sisters have hearts in their eyes.

"Ah, young love," Bristol says, her eyes glossing over with tears. She and her long-term boyfriend broke up last week, so I'm unsure if the tears are happy or sad.

Hannah puts her arm around her sister in a comforting gesture. Unlike me and Harrison, West and his sisters actually look alike. All with blonde hair and blue eyes.

"What date are you guys thinking for the wedding??" West's mom asks, rubbing her hands together excitedly. Her hair is now more grey than blonde, but you can still see the girls got their pretty features from her.

I glance at West. "Um, we haven't really had time to talk about it… since we just got engaged an hour ago."

She laughs and says, "True. Well, let me know if you need any help planning!"

My mom sidles up next to me and I wrap an arm around her shoulders. "I'll definitely need both of your help. So brace yourselves for being extra busy for the foreseeable future." They grin at each other, looking more than thrilled about the idea.

Once we've all toasted and celebrated, our family and friends leave, offering congratulations before they go. Harrison drove my car for me so I could ride home with West… my fiancé. My heart flutters at the thought.

West locks up the gorgeous cabin and we stand outside for a moment, staring at our new home.

"We should get married here," I tell him.

He looks from the house to me. "Really?"

I nod. "It would be perfect. We could have the ceremony out back in front of the lake."

West pulls me into his arms and kisses the top of my head. "I'd marry you anywhere, but I love that idea."

"We're going to have so many amazing memories here," I whisper against his chest.

He reaches a hand to my chin and tilts my head up to look at him. "We will. I can't wait to build a life with you, Melanie."

West kisses me soft, slow, and tender. Just like our story.

We happened slowly, starting in our tender teenaged years, and eventually... *finally*.... we ended up here.

In each other's arms.

Right where we belong.

ALSO BY LEAH BRUNNER

Check out Leah's other books! In book one you can read Madden and Odette Windell's love story!

LEAH'S LIT LOVERS
READER GROUP

Come join the fun in Leah's reader group! It's like a party. But you don't have to leave your house.

AND you don't want to miss the conversation and giveaways!

ACKNOWLEDGMENTS

Thank you to Melody Jeffries Design for my amazing cover, you really brought West and Mel to life!

A big thank you also to Amy Guan and Erin Packard for editing. You both brought vital insight to my manuscript and helped me turn it into a real book!

ABOUT THE AUTHOR

Leah Brunner is a military spouse currently residing with her family in Ohio. She and her husband have three adorable, (and sometimes crazy), children, and a Maine Coon cat.

As a child, Leah always dreamt of writing children's books about cats... but once she grew up (sort of) RomComs just felt right!

She strives to write realistic and relatable characters who feel like your best friends. And lots of witty banter to keep you laughing!

Made in the USA
Monee, IL
22 March 2025

14404106R00080